A Pirate in Distress

"Eddie's not a cousin, but he is a pirate," said Zelda.

Salem pushed himself up and rubbed his two front paws together in anticipation. His yellow eyes glowed. "Then we're talking gold and silver and precious gems. We're talking booty; we're talking treasure. Yee-hah!" He leaped from the table and scampered into the living room, his tail held high.

"If Eddie's not a cousin," Sabrina asked, "then what is he?"

"A friend," Zelda answered. "A very good and trusted friend."

"So what is he doing here?"

"That's what I'm waiting to hear. Eddie didn't just come from the Other Realm to chat. It's been almost three hundred years since I've seen him. I think he's in trouble. And if he came into the mortal realm to find me, it's got to be really big trouble."

Now there's a cheery thought, Sabrina told herself. Trouble that came from the Other Realm was always big. But what would it take for a pirate to think he was in trouble?

Sabrina, the Teenage Witch® books

Available from ARCHWAY Paperbacks

Pirate Pandemonium

Mel Odom

Based upon the characters in Archie Comics

**And based upon the television series
Sabrina, The Teenage Witch
Created for television by Nell Scovell
Developed for television by Jonathan Schmock**

AN ARCHWAY PAPERBACK
Published by POCKET BOOKS
New York   London   Toronto   Sydney   Singapore

This book is a work of fiction. Names, characters, places, and incidents are products of the author's imagination or are used fictitiously. Any resemblance to actual events or locales or persons, living or dead, is entirely coincidental.

AN ARCHWAY PAPERBACK *Original*

An Archway Paperback published by
POCKET BOOKS, a division of Simon & Schuster, Inc.
1230 Avenue of the Americas, New York, NY 10020

ISBN: 0-671-04072-3

First Archway Paperback printing February 2001

10 9 8 7 6 5 4 3 2 1

AN ARCHWAY PAPERBACK and colophon are registered trademarks of Simon & Schuster, Inc.

SABRINA THE TEENAGE WITCH and all related titles, logos and characters are trademarks of Archie Comics Publications, Inc.

Printed in the U.S.A.

IL 4+

This book is for my daughter, Montana, who has one of the prettiest smiles in the whole world and has learned to love the world of drama.

And for Ingrid van der Leeden, who is gracious enough to let me continue playing around in the wonderful world that is Sabrina, the Teenage Witch.

Pirate Pandemonium

Chapter 1

☆

"**S**abrina Spellman, don't you dare!"

Frozen in midpoint with a magic spell on her lips, Sabrina sheepishly glanced over at her aunt Zelda. *How is it that even in a crowded mall, a parent figure always knows when you're about to do something maybe a little less than right?*

A tough, shop-till-you-drop Saturday morning crowd filled Westbridge Mall, circling the concourse. Most people seemed lost in the confusion. But Zelda had spotted Sabrina's slight hand movement even from the furniture shop across the mall on the other side of the spraying fountain.

Sabrina put her hand behind her head and smoothed her blond hair, trying her best to appear innocent. She wore a salmon halter top, white Capri pants, and white sandals, her hair done up in a fishtail braid. *No one could look more innocent.* "Me? I wasn't doing anything." *See? I even sound innocent.*

1

Zelda crossed the concourse and looked at Sabrina with disapproval. She was blond and slender, dressed in a navy blouse and khaki slacks. "And what exactly was it you weren't about to do?" She folded her arms and waited.

Sabrina felt kind of awful. Nobody did guilt better than Aunt Zelda. Where Aunt Hilda sometimes looked the other way or handed out mild punishment, Zelda practiced more along the straight and narrow.

"It's Harvey," Sabrina explained, caving.

"What about him?"

"Remember when I told you his dad's pesticide business was going through a slump and Harvey had to get a job at the mall?"

"Yes, but I don't see what that has to do with using your magic so openly in the mall."

"That's because you haven't seen the job." Sabrina pointed at the food court in the intersection ahead. Actually, she didn't think she was using her magic openly. Her spell would have been hidden. Since going to live with her aunts at the age of sixteen and learning that she was a witch with fantastic powers, she'd learned a lot about using her magic.

Especially the not getting caught part.

People filled the food court. Stands sold hot dogs, pretzels, ice cream, pizza, Chinese takeout, tacos, and more under neon signs. All the tables in the center area were filled, so most of the patrons wandered off juggling food. Kids with colorful helium-filled balloons given out by the mall remained in orbit around their parents, adding to the general confusion.

However, while most of the food stands stayed busy, Ye Olde Doges didn't. A group of boys Sabrina recognized from Westbridge High had formed a heckling ring at the corn dog stand. Their target was the food stand attendant dressed as a basset hound with an oversized head and a floppy chef's hat.

"Hey, pooch," one of the hecklers called out, "I'll bet you're really smart. Can you tell me what grows on the outside of trees?"

The basset hound's shoulders slumped, and Sabrina knew the guy inside the suit had just sighed.

"I don't think he knows, Gerry," another heckler said.

"Sure he does." Gerry smiled wickedly. "C'mon, fleabag, bark for us. The answer is bark. Bark grows on the outside of trees."

All the hecklers laughed like it was the funniest thing they'd heard. Gerry Naylor was one of the biggest and most popular guys on the Westbridge High Fighting Scallions football team. A lot of kids wanted to make sure Gerry had a good time whenever he was around. Gerry in a bad mood was a scary thing.

"Let me guess," Zelda said. "That's Harvey in the dog costume."

"Yes," Sabrina replied unhappily. Harvey Kinkle was the love of her life even though he wasn't a star football player or a great student. There was just something so . . . so . . . *Harveyish* about him. She hated seeing him treated this way, but the hecklers were merciless.

"I can understand why you'd feel like pointing up something annoying," Zelda said.

"It would only be a teeny one," Sabrina wheedled. "I wouldn't even call it annoying. Distracting, that's more like what I had in mind."

"I got an easier one, pooch," Gerry said. He was big and buff in his varsity jacket. He leaned over the counter. "Can you tell me what's on top of a house?"

Harvey the Basset Hound folded his arms, his paw gloves flopping. He shook his too-big head and looked totally mournful.

"Roof!" Gerry barked. "Roof! Roof!" He laughed and slapped the counter. "Roof! Get it? That's what's on top of a house."

The crowd of hecklers laughed again. Some of them slapped Gerry on the back and encouraged him.

"Harvey shouldn't have to go through this," Sabrina said.

"I agree." Obviously displeased, Zelda looked around. "Have you seen mall security? Perhaps they could do something."

The diners at the food court stayed away from Ye Olde Doges.

"I didn't see them," Sabrina replied.

Gerry took a fistful of mustard packages from a plastic bucket on the counter. He lined them up on the counter pointing at Harvey.

"Hey," Harvey said, stepping forward. "Don't do that, Gerry."

The big football player only laughed. "Fire one!"

Then he brought his hand down hard on the back of the mustard package.

The mustard squirted through the other end of the package like a cannon blast. Gooey, yellow mustard sprayed over Harvey's hound dog face and dripped from his muzzle. He rushed forward, holding his hands up. "Stop!"

Gerry hit the next mustard packet. The contents squirted the soda machine beside Harvey.

"Enough is enough," Zelda said, pointing.

The next mustard packet Gerry slapped exploded under his hand and splattered all over his varsity jacket. The yellow looked garish against the green and white team colors.

"Oh man," one of the other guys said. "Look at your jacket, Gerry."

Mortified, Gerry grabbed a napkin from the counter and wiped at the mustard furiously. The wiping only spread the mustard. He threw the napkin down. "This is all your fault, Kinkle! Now you're going to get creamed!" He put his hands on the countertop, ready to jump over.

Sabrina pointed at the line of mustard packets. She murmured,

Okay, this has gotten out of hand,
And now it's really scary.
Fire one, fire two, and fire three
To splatter the hecklers and Gerry.

The mustard packets suddenly erupted like

popping corn. Lines of mustard shot through the air like Silly String and coated Gerry and his buddies. There was a stunned moment of silence, then the hecklers wailed in angry disbelief.

"You're going to get it now, Kinkle!" someone roared.

The crowd at the food court backed away. Parents grabbed their small children and hustled them back into the main mall area. Balloons that escaped from the startled kids' hands shot up like emergency flares.

Harvey raised his paws as the hecklers started for him. "Hey, I didn't do anything."

Sabrina knew that was true, but it wasn't going to matter. She looked around desperately, hoping for some inspiration.

"You boys hold it right there!" a stern voice commanded.

Sabrina recognized the voice at once. She glanced up the escalator that led down from the main mall floor. "Mr. Kraft."

Willard Kraft was the principal at Westbridge High. He wore a brown suit jacket and slacks, but sported a chocolate turtleneck instead of a shirt and tie. Fair-haired and sallow-complexioned, Mr. Kraft didn't look like much of a threat, but he handed out detention slips with a speed that beat most fast food drive-thrus.

"Miss Spellman," Mr. Kraft acknowledged as he stepped off the escalator. Then he caught sight of

Zelda. His shoulders squared, and he gave her a jaunty salute. "Zelda."

"Hello, Willard," Zelda said warmly.

"It's good to see you, Zelda," Mr. Kraft said, his eyes twinkling. "I'll speak further to you in a moment. As soon as I attend to this ruckus." The principal squared his shoulders again and walked through the food court crowd to the mustard-spattered hecklers.

"Of course, Willard." Zelda had a goofy smile on her face that made Sabrina queasy.

I do not know how she can care for someone so obnoxious, Sabrina thought. Mr. Kraft's relationship with her aunt was a mystery to her and Aunt Hilda. Hilda had dated Willard first, but they'd had absolutely nothing in common. However, now that Mr. Kraft was interested in Zelda, Hilda was a little jealous of the attention he paid her sister. Their dating made nights at the Spellman household a little uncomfortable at times.

"What's going on?" Hilda asked as she joined them. Where her sister was notoriously conservative in appearance and opinion, Hilda was a free spirit. She wore a brightly colored gypsy dress with a long hem and a matching kerchief around her hair.

The ensemble fit Hilda's flashy personality perfectly, but Sabrina knew she'd also worn it to annoy Zelda. The sisters were at the mall to look at new living room furniture, and their outfits represented the opposite taste they had in furniture as well.

Sabrina pointed at the basset hound at Ye Olde Doges counter. "That's Harvey."

"Oh." Hilda took in the mustard-speckled football players. "And the crash-course in condiments?"

"Me," Sabrina admitted.

Hilda smiled, deepening her dimples. "Not bad." She started to point. "But you could have used a little—"

Zelda grabbed her sister's finger. "No."

"No?" Hilda frowned.

Zelda still wore her goofy smile. "No, Willard's got everything well in hand."

Mr. Kraft strode through the food court diners. "Excuse me, excuse me. Principal coming through."

"Oh," Hilda said with a total lack of enthusiasm, "so Willard the Wonder Boy is going to play the hero."

"Yes," Zelda replied, holding her hands together. "He has such a commanding presence, don't you think?"

Actually, Sabrina thought the diners looked at Mr. Kraft like he was an alien.

"Pardon me if I gag," Hilda stated. "It's just one of those automatic muscle reflexes. Like applying electricity to a frog's leg."

"Principal," Mr. Kraft blustered again. "Principal coming through. Thank you."

Gerry and his fellow hecklers stared at Mr. Kraft in disbelief. The principal halted in front of the boys. He looked small against the football players. The diners cleared out around Mr. Kraft and the football players as if an Old West gunfight were about to start. Mr. Kraft watched them go, then suddenly looked a little nervous.

Gerry glared at the principal. "It's Saturday. School's out."

Swallowing hard, Mr. Kraft waved a finger in Gerry's face. "You listen to me, young man. Don't think I can't hand out detention on a Saturday."

Gerry brushed at the mustard on his jacket. "I'm the leading defensive linebacker in our division. Coach wouldn't think much of you giving me detention for something I did on a Saturday."

"Your coach," Mr. Kraft declared, reaching inside his jacket and taking out a detention slip pad, "will listen to me."

A sarcastic smile on his face, Gerry shrugged and said, "If Coach does, I bet my dad doesn't."

Mr. Kraft's pencil lead broke, and he swallowed hard. Gerry's dad was a well-known criminal lawyer.

"I don't know law like my dad," Gerry went on, "but I bet there's some kind of law against principals stalking students."

Mr. Kraft's hand shook a little. His smile suddenly looked way too tight. "Perhaps I was just a bit hasty."

"You think?"

Mr. Kraft held his thumb and forefinger a fraction of an inch apart. This time his smile looked painful. "Maybe a little."

"Hero to zero," Hilda whispered, "in under three seconds. It's a new record."

"His heart was in the right place," Zelda said, shooting her sister a reproachful glare. "He's just a little out of his depth. He needs a little support."

Hilda raised her finger, ready to point.

"No," Zelda said, starting through the crowd that was watching the spectacle. "Not a spell. He needs someone at his side."

Going over there is not a good idea, Sabrina thought, but she knew she couldn't stop her aunt.

Harvey took off the basset hound head. "Hey, Gerry, Mr. Kraft was just—"

"Who said you could get out of your kennel, Fido?" Gerry demanded.

"Nobody," Harvey said. "I just think that talking to the school principal like that is kind of rude."

Sabrina felt a flush of pride. "That's my Harvey," she told Hilda. "Always thinking of other people." It was only one of dozens of things she liked about him.

"That," Hilda pointed out, "is a personality defect that will get your head put on the chopping block with everybody else's. Vengeance the stealth-point way is best."

Zelda made her way through the crowd and was closing in on Mr. Kraft.

"I think the way he talked to me is kind of rude. I mean, he did admit he was being hasty. Or was that"—Gerry grabbed the ketchup squirt bottle from the corn dog counter—"tasty?" He squeezed ketchup from the bottle, hosing Mr. Kraft's face and jacket.

Mr. Kraft froze, his face livid enough to almost match the ketchup. Both his glasses lenses were covered.

"Willard!" Zelda gasped as she reached the principal's side.

"Look, Gerry," one of the hecklers said, laughing as he pointed at Zelda. "Bonus points!"

Gerry turned the ketchup bottle toward Zelda and grinned menacingly. Zelda stopped at Mr. Kraft's side.

Hilda shifted at Sabrina's side. "Well, this should certainly be interesting."

"Shouldn't we stop this?" Sabrina asked.

"No," Hilda replied. "I think we'll let Zelda handle this. She did tell us to stay out of it. More or less. And Harvey's safe for the moment."

Zelda stood at her full height and took Mr. Kraft's arm. "I don't think you want to do that."

Gerry pulled the ketchup bottle back and looked at it more closely. Then he shook his head. "Nope. I'm pretty sure I *do* want to do it." He pointed the ketchup bottle again and prepared to squirt.

A sudden, thunderous voice filled the food court. "Avast there with that bilge, ye knock-kneed, pigeon-toed landlubber! If'n ye touch a hair on that girlie's fair head, I'll keelhaul and feed ye to the fishes, I will! I give ye me promise on that!"

Gerry froze and looked up.

Sabrina looked up, too. The speaker had the attention of everyone in the food court, as well as several of the people standing around the railing on the floor above.

The speaker leaned over the railing and glared down with one eye. He looked like a giant, easily topping six and a half feet in height. A black patch covered the other eye. Beneath his dusty tricorn hat, his face was craggy, partially covered by the thick black beard and mustache, and it looked like it had been chopped into shape with a dulled axe. He wore stained cream-colored leather breeches tucked into knee-high rolled-top boots and a ratty-looking crimson blouse with a ruffled front and sleeves hacked off at the shoulder. A ragged black cape hung to his boot tops. Bold dark blue and black tattoos covered his sun-browned arms. Gold hoops hung from his ears.

"Wow," Hilda said, smiling.

Sabrina looked at her aunt. " 'Wow'? *Wow* is all you have to say? Westbridge Mall has just been invaded by pirates, and all you can say is *Wow?*"

"Wow," Hilda repeated. Her grin had gotten bigger. "You know, I'd forgotten how cute freebooters could be."

"Cute?" Sabrina exploded. "May I remind you that this is the mortal realm. We don't have pirates here."

"We have hackers," Hilda argued. "They're cyber-pirates."

"We don't have pirates like that," Sabrina said, pointing to the big man.

"No," Hilda said wistfully. "They don't make them like that anymore, do they?"

Sabrina blew out her breath in exasperation. "Aunt Zelda must have pointed him up. What could she have been thinking?"

Gerry looked sullen by the corn dog stand. "Who do you think you are, tough guy?" He waved the ketchup bottle menacingly. "Why don't you come down here and say that?"

Quick as a wink, the pirate threw himself over the railing's edge. His cape fluttered behind him. His boots smacked when he landed in a half-crouch.

Sabrina couldn't believe it. *A normal guy would have broken both legs with a jump like that. Then again, dressed like that, he can't be a normal guy.*

The pirate grinned, lips rolling back to expose a gold capped tooth in the form of a skull. "I'm Black Edwin Peas, ye little gout o' foul air, fiercest pirate in these here parts. Ye'll do well to remember that." He strode forward, drawing a curved cutlass from his broad belt. Silver and gold bracelets gleamed on his forearms and biceps. A belt across his chest held a brace of flintlock pistols.

Gerry stood his ground, but his friends all backed away. He wasn't even aware of it.

The pirate swung his cutlass in a glittering arc. The halves of the ketchup bottle fell in different directions. Red tomato slime covered Gerry's hand as a look of terror filled his face.

"If'n I can do that to that jug of yers," the pirate roared, brandishing his cutlass, "imagine what I can do to that great melon of a head ye got."

Gerry backed away, trying to save face. "Hey, pirate dude, just take it easy. My dad's a lawyer, and he won't—"

"A lawyer, is he?" the pirate roared, then guffawed. "Why, ye see, I don't much care for lawyers, ye little obnoxious squirt. Last one I met, why, I left him

13

a-hangin' from the yardarm of my ship till the gulls picked his bones clean. They ain't as partic'lar as me."

Yuck! Sabrina thought, instantly losing the snack appetite she'd been building up.

Gerry paled. Then he turned and ran, and his crowd ran after him.

"That's right, ye ungainly little popinjays," the pirate taunted. "Run them stumpy little legs of yers afore ye really make me mad."

Thinking about the long jump the pirate had just done, Sabrina had to wonder what the big man was capable of when he was angry.

The pirate sheathed his sword, the keen edge rasping against his leather belt in the silence that covered the food court. He glared, narrowing his one good eye at the diners. "Well, ye great lummoxes, ye a-gonna stand there or are ye a-gonna eat?"

The food court cleared as quickly as the escalators and stairways would allow.

Then the pirate turned back to Zelda. "Well blow me down and call me an old salty dog. If'n it isn't me old shipmate, Zellie Spellman. I knowed it was ye. Woulda knowed ye if it'd been six hundred years instead of the last three hundred it's been."

Zellie? Sabrina thought. *Shipmate?*

"Well, don't ye remember me, girlie?" the pirate demanded. "Or are ye a-gonna tell me ye plumb forgot me after all them times I saved yer life?"

Zelda smiled. "Hello, Eddie."

Sabrina's jaw dropped. *Eddie!?*

Chapter 2

☆

☆

"And as I recall," Zelda said, "I saved your life more than you saved mine."

"Ah, ye never were no good at cipherin'," Eddie the pirate said.

"I was always the best at math," Zelda objected. "Why else did Captain Cutter put me in charge of splitting the treasure we took?"

" 'Cause ye always cleaned up better'n the rest of the crew." Eddie shook his head sadly and wiped at his eye. "An' look at ye now. A-keepin' score on who saved who most. Breaks me ol' heart, it does." He took out a dirty handkerchief and honked like a goose.

"Fine," Zelda said. "We're even."

"C'mere, girlie," Eddie said, beaming and holding his brawny arms out. "Give us a hug."

Mr. Kraft stepped in front of Zelda protectively.

"She is most certainly not going to do that." He drew himself up to his full height.

Eddie put his fists on his hips and thrust his big face forward. "An' what are ye gonna do about it? Threaten me with detention, too? Why, if'n I was to tell you what I did to me old schoolmaster back in third grade, why ye'd tuck yer tail between yer legs and head for open water quick as the wind would blow ye."

Sabrina continued watching in disbelief. "Who is this guy?" she asked Hilda.

"I don't know," Hilda replied. "He hasn't attacked. He must be a friend of Zelda's."

"I didn't know she had friends like this." Sabrina watched the pirate, noticing Harvey slipping over the corn dog counter. "I mean, ones with swords and pistols and tall boots and a gold skull on his tooth."

"I know," Hilda said. "Surprising, isn't it? And he's so cute!"

Sabrina didn't see cute.

"I'm not afraid of you," Mr. Kraft protested bravely.

Eddie bent his head closer, then said gruffly, "Boo!"

Mr. Kraft said, "Eeeep!" and dashed behind Zelda.

The pirate let loose a great belly laugh that Sabrina couldn't help thinking would have gone great with a Santa Claus costume. *As long as you like Santa wearing an eyepatch.*

"Eddie," Zelda said, "stop it."

The pirate grinned. "Just havin' a little fun, girlie.

Let me get a good look at you." He reached up and turned up his eyepatch, revealing another twinkling sea green eye. He caught up Zelda's hands in his massive paws. "Oh, an' ye're a sight for sore eyes, girlie, that ye are."

Zelda looked slightly embarrassed. She got even more embarrassed when Eddie swept her into a fierce bear hug and lifted her feet from the ground, but she hugged the big man back.

"Put me down, you great blundering behemoth," Zelda ordered.

Gently, Eddie put Zelda back on her feet. "Of course, of course. Glad to see ye ain't gone soft none, Zellie."

"I'm a little more settled these days," Zelda said.

The pirate frowned. "Settling down's not for me, girlie. Give me a fair wind an' an open sea to make me happy. Only place I care to be is a place I never been, where cargo ships are fat with treasure and no ship's fast enough to catch me."

"Same old Eddie," Zelda said.

"Aye," the pirate promised. "Till the day they drop me in Davy Jones's locker."

"Maybe," Mr. Kraft said from behind Zelda, "they can drop you in jail for a while first."

Sabrina followed the principal's gaze up the escalator. A small knot of Westbridge Mall security officers gathered uncertainly at the top.

"All right, buddy," one of the guards said. "I'm Sergeant Taylor. Put down the sword and pistols. Get on your knees and put your hands behind your head."

"I'll not be doing that today," Eddie declared sternly. He fisted his cutlass and pulled it out. "I'm a free man, an' I intend on staying that way."

"We can do this the hard way," Sergeant Taylor said, leading his men down the escalator.

Eddie only grinned bigger as he faced Zelda. "C'mon, girlie. Fetch yer sword and let's have at these king's men. It'll be like old times."

Sabrina's heart was in her mouth. Ever since she'd gotten her witch powers, her aunts had emphasized the need to keep them secret. The sudden appearance of a pirate in a crowded mall in the real world wasn't covered in the Magic Handbook or anything her aunts had taught her. They were all about to get seriously busted.

"Officer, wait," Zelda said calmly, stepping forward. "There's been a mistake. You see, my cousin Edwin Peas is an actor. He's here to promote Ye Olde Doges food stand."

"He is?" Harvey asked, carrying the basset hound head under his arm. He smiled. "That's cool, but I wish they'd told me."

"He's an actor?" the security sergeant repeated doubtfully. His hands never left the handcuffs and walkie-talkie at his belt. He glanced at the corn dog stand. "Looks like they're more into a Bowser type of look."

"Actually," Zelda said, "that type of promotion isn't working out at all."

"Tell me about it," Harvey added, nodding. "I've

18

been sitting here all morning. Heat up corn dogs, throw them away. And this suit is really hot."

"An actor?" Sergeant Taylor asked again.

Eddie glanced at Zelda, then back at the security officer. "Aye. That be right. Came here to earn an honest day's pay, I did."

"And your act involved menacing a bunch of high school kids with that sword?" the security sergeant asked.

"Those kids," Mr. Kraft said, pushing his glasses up on his nose as he stepped from behind Zelda, "were a menace. They were heckling poor Harvey—that's him in the dog suit—and, well," he said, waving at his suit jacket and glasses, "you can see what they did to me."

"I see." The security sergeant faced Eddie again with an intensity that convinced Sabrina they weren't going to get away with it. "And what was your act?"

"A short act from Gilbert and Sullivan," Zelda said.

"I don't know anything about Gilbert and Sullivan," Sergeant Taylor said.

"Shakespeare," a security guard behind him said. "Something to do with plays and stuff."

Sabrina looked up and saw the mall crowd gathering around the railing. The potential for disaster was getting greater than ever. And she still had no clue who Eddie Peas was or what he was doing there.

"Shakespeare," Sergeant Taylor repeated doubtfully, watching the other guard nod. He turned back to Eddie. "Okay, Shakespeare, let's see some of your work."

For the first time, fear touched the big pirate's face. "You want me to sing and dance?" he croaked.

"If that's what this Gilbert and Sullivan stuff is about," the security sergeant said, "then, yep, that's exactly what I want."

Eddie looked up at the crowd around the railing. He actually paled, and perspiration beaded on his forehead. "In front of them?"

"Yep." The security sergeant was relentless.

Eddie glanced at Zelda, who nodded encouragement. Eddie hooked a finger at his shirt collar. He cleared his throat.

We're sunk! Sabrina thought grimly.

Instead, Eddie began an intricate set of steps, hands held high as he turned sharply, then did a jig. And then he sang in that deep voice of his.

When I sally forth to seek my prey
I help myself in a royal way.
I sink a few more ships, it's true,
Than a well-bred monarch ought to do;
But many a king on a first-class throne,
If he wants to call his crown his own,
Must manage somehow to get through
More dirty work than e'er I do,
For I am a Pirate King!
And it is, it is a glorious thing
To be a Pirate King!
For I am a Pirate King!

Eddie stopped his jig and swept his tricorn hat off with a flourish. He bowed deeply.

His voice, Sabrina suddenly realized, was unexpectedly beautiful.

The crowd above began clapping enthusiastically, and Zelda clapped loudest of all. Even Sergeant Taylor seemed a little more at ease. "Okay, Shakespeare, let me see that sword and those pistols."

Gingerly, Eddie pulled the sword from his belt and offered it hilt first to the security sergeant. Sabrina held her breath, knowing there was no way the acting excuse was going to explain the sword or the pistols.

Zelda pointed discreetly.

When the security sergeant waved the sword, the thick blade wobbled. Sergeant Taylor poked the sword at the floor, and the blade bent. He took one of Eddie's flintlock pistols, examined it briefly, then pointed it into the air and pulled the trigger.

Sabrina rammed her fingers into her ears, expecting a loud report. Instead, the pistol gave a fizzling little pop, and out plopped a flag on a stick. When the flag unfurled, it read BANG!

The security sergeant grinned and handed the weapons back to Eddie. "A rubber sword and gimmicked pistols aren't really a smart thing to bring into a mall."

"Aye," Eddie replied, waving the rubbery sword in perplexity. "I's just a-doin' what I was told, sir."

"Maybe you could just tone it down a little."

"Aye, sir. I'll see to that right quick."

The security sergeant glanced at Mr. Kraft. "Do you know the boys who did this?"

"Yes," Mr. Kraft said.

"If you're willing to swear out a complaint, we should be able to do something about their behavior."

Enthusiasm gleamed in Mr. Kraft's eyes. "You have forms? Police forms?"

"Incident report forms."

Mr. Kraft smiled. "That sounds close enough." He took a napkin from the counter and wiped at the ketchup covering his jacket. "Well, lead on, Macduff." He looked back at Zelda and smiled uncertainly. "Shakespeare kind of rubs off on you, doesn't it?"

Eddie the pirate scowled at Mr. Kraft. "That's 'Lay on, Macduff,' you great pointy-eared ninny."

Mr. Kraft shook his finger at Eddie but quickly yanked it back when the pirate snapped at it and growled like a rabid dog. Eddie roared with laughter.

"Hey, Mr. Pirate," a young boy called down from above.

"Aye, lad," Eddie called back up, looking a little surprised. "And what is it ye'd be wanting after?"

"Can I get your autograph? I never got an autograph from a pirate before."

"Well sure ye can, lad. I'd be right proud to doodle up an autograph for ye."

The boy started down the escalator, neatly avoiding his mom's reach. In seconds, dozens of other kids joined him, becoming a boiling mass of excitement by the time they reached the bottom of the escalator.

Sabrina watched, totally amazed at the way the big pirate seemed to fit right in with the kids. They instantly took to him, crawling up in his arms and pulling at his beard. Despite the distractions, Eddie cleared a table and set up chairs, then caught Zelda's eye.

"Zellie, ye don't mind if I humor the little tykes a bit now, do ye?" the pirate asked as he sat down.

"No," Zelda answered. "This seems to be your party."

Eddie grinned broadly. "Ah, an' I knew ye bein' a right fine girlie and not a bad pirate yerself that ye'd understand."

Sabrina moved over to Zelda and whispered, "You were a pirate?"

"Not really."

"He thinks you were."

"Well, it was nothing really. It only lasted for that one summer." Zelda pointed up a stack of eight-by-ten glossies. They showed Eddie standing in front of a Jolly Roger with his cutlass raised and a huge grin on his face. A green parrot perched on his shoulder.

"One summer?" Sabrina asked incredulously, but Zelda joined Eddie at the table with the pictures and an old-fashioned quill and inkwell.

"Thank ye," the pirate said to Zelda, and he set to autographing as if it were something he did every day.

"The corn dogs have a neat surprise in them

today," Zelda said. "The sticks inside them are shaped like pirates." Several members of the crowd went over to place their orders.

Frustrated and feeling totally lost, her mind spinning, Sabrina noticed that Harvey was suddenly swamped at the counter. She hurried over to help him.

"Boy," Harvey said as he loaded more corn dogs into the microwaves on the back shelf of the food stand, "if I'd known the company was going to do this kind of a promotion, I'd have been better prepared."

"Let me do that," Sabrina said. "You take care of the cash register." She started loading the corn dogs into the microwaves.

"Sure." Harvey started taking orders and calling them out.

Sabrina worked quickly. Thankfully Hilda joined her, and they dealt with the crowd quickly. But the whole time Sabrina's mind kept focusing on the fact that Zelda had once been a pirate. It was really hard to imagine.

Sabrina watched as the last customer walked away from the corn dog stand. In the last forty-five minutes, she'd lost count of how many corn dogs she'd served with mustard, ketchup, and ranch dressing. Her hair had also died from the steamy heat given off by the microwaves, slithering free of the braid she'd so carefully pointed up, hanging now in limp strands.

"Wow," Harvey said, smiling. "We're going to

have to have that pirate guy here more often. I don't think I've ever seen so many corn dogs in my life."

"Me neither," Sabrina agreed. "I don't think I want to ever see another corn dog."

"I don't know," Harvey said. "I kind of like them. I just didn't know they had the pirate sticks in them. I mean, the two I had this morning didn't."

Sabrina knew Zelda had magically changed the corn dog sticks. "You must have gotten the last two."

"I suppose I did. Pretty lucky, huh?"

"Yes." Sabrina helped him finish wiping the counter down.

"Hey, I really appreciate all the help, Sab," he said, using his pet name for her. "I couldn't have done it without you. Or you, Hilda."

Hilda smiled as she left the food stand. "You're welcome, Harvey."

Harvey took a deep breath. "Man, I'm bushed."

"Hey," Sabrina said, "I thought we had a date tonight. You and me. Movie and the Slicery. Ring any bells?"

"Sure." Harvey yawned. "I'll be rested by then." He shook his head as he looked at Zelda and Black Edwin Peas. "I can't believe your aunt's cousin is a pirate."

Sabrina watched the man talking animatedly with her aunt. "Me neither. Who knew?"

"Okay," Sabrina said, walking into the kitchen at the Spellman house, "I kind of gathered from the way Cousin Eddie was gawking at all the streets and buildings on the way back from the mall that he's not from around here."

Zelda pointed up a tea service. The aroma of spiced tea filled the air.

"Cousin Eddie?" Salem asked as he woke from a nap on the kitchen table. At present, Salem Saberhagen was a black shorthaired American cat, but he'd once been a powerful warlock. The Witches' Council had turned him into a cat for a hundred years for almost taking over the world in the mortal realm. "Which Cousin Eddie?"

"He's not from around here," Zelda said as she searched the cabinets for cups. "He's from the Other Realm."

Sabrina nodded. She'd expected that. The Other Realm was where a lot of witches and other magical creatures lived away from the mortal realm. Of course, there were a lot of ways to get from one realm to the other, including the upstairs linen closet in the Spellman house.

"Which Cousin Eddie?" Salem whined. "If it's Cousin Eddie Feldman, he may not be happy to see me." Salem paused. "Of course, I could be even less happy than I am. How was I supposed to know after I turned him into a duck-billed platypus that I'd be turned into a cat by the Witches' Council and lose my powers?"

"He's really a pirate?" Sabrina asked, ignoring the cat.

"Yes." Zelda arranged the chosen cups on the silver tray.

Salem's eyes got round. "Cousin Eddie Feldman is a pirate?"

Zelda sighed and looked at the cat. "It's not Cousin Eddie Feldman."

"Good," the cat replied. "You don't know how many nightmares I've had of running away from a duck-billed platypus. It's always like those old mummy movies. The duck-billed platypus moves incredibly slow, but somehow Cousin Eddie just remained right there, that big beak open while those webbed feet went *slap-huh-slap-huh-slap!*"

"And you were a pirate for a summer?" Sabrina asked.

"Yes." Zelda didn't really want to talk much about that summer.

"You were a pirate?" Salem shook his head in dismay. "And the Witches' Council thought I was the bad one."

"You *were* the bad one," Zelda said. "I was a pirate for a summer. You were a pirate for years."

"Oh," Salem said, "you knew about that."

"I'm on the Witches' Council," Zelda reminded him. "I ended up knowing more about you than I ever wanted to."

"Then you know why—if that's Cousin Eddie Ackroyd—I don't want to see him."

"It's not Cousin Eddie Ackroyd," Zelda responded. "And I do know why, and I still can't believe you did that."

"I was weak," Salem moaned. "I couldn't stop

myself. I needed help. I was greedy, but I've changed. And tentacles aren't really a bad look."

"He's not a cousin at all." Zelda got milk from the refrigerator and added a bag of scones to the tray.

"But he is a pirate?" Sabrina asked.

"Yes."

"We're not talking baseball here, are we?" Salem asked.

"No." Zelda picked up the tray.

"Or software?" Salem pressed.

"No."

Salem pushed himself up and rubbed his two front paws together in anticipation. His yellow eyes glowed. "Then we're talking gold and silver and precious gems. We're talking booty; we're talking treasure. Yee-hah!" He leaped from the table and scampered into the living room, his tail held high.

"If he's not a cousin," Sabrina asked, "then what is he?"

"A friend," Zelda answered. "A very good and trusted friend."

"So what is he doing here?"

"That's what I'm waiting to hear." Zelda carried the tea service toward the door. "Eddie didn't just come from the Other Realm to chat. It's been almost three hundred years since I've seen him. Since he's here now, I'm betting he thinks he has a really good reason."

"He's had plenty of time to tell you."

"You have to know Eddie. He doesn't get around to a story till he's ready." She hesitated. "I think he's in trouble. And if he came into the mortal realm to find me, it's got to be really big trouble."

Now there's a cheery thought, Sabrina told herself. Trouble that came from the Other Realm was always big. But what would it take for a pirate to think he was in trouble?

it's too hard to send it to earth now the metal is always leaving Earth to get to the really big trouble.

Now I gotta leave," Sabrina said. Sabrina told him, said. "I mean, I did come here, but since Reading was always big. You mean, would it be I've gotta go to

☆

Chapter 3

☆

"So there we was in that dark alley," Black Eddie Peas said in a quiet voice that carried easily to his listeners in the Spellman living room. "Just Cap'n Cutter, Zellie, and me, an' us havin' the king's jewels in a serving wench's stocking while an army was searchin' for us." The pirate sprawled on the couch, managing to take up every bit of available space except where Salem perched on one arm.

Hilda and Zelda sat in recliners, hanging on every word.

"You escaped the king's guard?" Sabrina sat on the floor, her arms wrapped around her knees. The floor had become uncomfortable an hour ago, but she hadn't had the willpower to get up and leave. The pirate's stories continued to be fascinating.

Eddie drank from the pewter ale mug he'd hauled out of his pack when Zelda had offered tea. The cup showed dents and dings from many years of wear and tear. EDDIE PEAS was inscribed in a childish scrawl on one side.

"Well, girlie," the pirate said, wiping his lips with the back of his arm, "ye see, we only thought we had. Them boys was onto us by the time we reached that alley. On us like the starving leeches they was. Cap'n Cutter, why he'd taken the lead, him knowing the ways of the city, of course. Me and Zellie, why we just followed."

Sabrina listened intently. During the last two hours, Eddie had spun tale after tale of derring-do and piracy aboard the high seas of at least a dozen different areas in the Other Realm. Several of them had included her aunt as a daring buccaneer.

"So what was in the treasure?" Salem demanded. "The suspense is killing me."

Eddie looked at the cat and laughed. "Well, you greedy varmint, ain't you worried about all them king's men we had a-breathin' down our necks?"

Salem thought for a moment. "No. I want to know what was in the box from the royal treasury. Kings keep all the really good stuff."

"Aye, that they do," Eddie agreed. "But, you see, I hadn't looked in that box yet. So I didn't know."

Salem groaned in frustration and looked at Zelda.

"Don't look at me, Salem," Zelda said. "One of the first rules you learn about being a pirate is to never interfere with another pirate's story. If you were ever any kind of pirate, you should know that."

"I *was* a pirate," Salem protested. "And the first rule of any pirate is to get the treasure."

Personally, Sabrina would have liked to hurry Eddie up. There was that date with Harvey only a few hours away. But the pirate's stories had captivated her. The present one included enough tricks and traps and court intrigues to fill ten Indiana Jones movies.

"Back to the alley," Sabrina said.

Eddie grinned at her. "Ah, girlie, ye remind me old heart of yer dear aunt back in them days. She was a right and proper fireball back then."

"Zelda?" Hilda looked skeptical.

"Aye," Eddie replied fondly. "Ye should have seen her like I seen her afore. Her hair, like fine gold it was, a-hangin' down, and her a-steppin' through cannon smoke thick as pea soup just a-wavin' her sword and a-darin' them blackhearts to come at her."

"Eddie," Zelda said, "now that's quite enough of that. I don't want to go give the wrong impression."

"Oh, an' there weren't no wrong impressions, girlie. Them pirates what ye dared, they know what you was about and that ye meant it."

Zelda frowned and glanced meaningfully at Sabrina.

Eddie coughed in embarrassment. "Aye, an' right ye are, Zellie." The pirate took another sip of tea and leaned forward, his elbows resting on his knees. "So there we were, in that alley what was dark as a shadow in a cemetery on a moonless night."

Sabrina listened, feeling a chill draw goose bumps on her arms.

Eddie continued, lowering his voice. "We heard the king's men a-cussin' 'cause they was thinkin' they was goin' to lose us," he said, "an' we heard 'em a-fretting 'cause they was a-feared they was a-gonna find us." He smiled. "An' there was but only the three of us."

"And the treasure," Salem put in, his tail waving hypnotically.

"Aye, an' the treasure."

"The king's men followed you into the alley?" Sabrina asked.

"No, girlie," Eddie said. "At first, we thought they did, sure enough. But them guards got ahead of us instead in all the confusion. Must have been a hundred of them, all a-bristlin' with swords and muskets. They blocked the alley slick as goose grease, cut off our way back to the ship. It didn't take us a minute to see that there wasn't no way out that way." He drank more tea. "Well, we seen what dire straits we was in, an' we knew we couldn't take all them king's men on, so we ran back to the other end of the alley. Only by the time we got there, another group of king's men—more'n a hundred of 'em, I'm here to tell ye—blocked that end of the alley, too."

Salem's tail paused. "Let me guess. You went up the fire escape?"

"Nope. Weren't no fire escapes, nor ladders neither."

Salem pushed himself up on his front paws. "You entered the buildings?"

Eddie shook his head. "Uh-uh. Weren't no doorways or windows to go through. I looked."

"There was no way out?" Salem asked in disbelief.

"None," Eddie replied solemnly. "Well," he continued conspiratorially, warming to his story, "I drew me cutlass. The cap'n, he drew his. And Zellie drew hers. Together, we stared down at them king's men as they closed in on us. An' let me tell ye now, whiskers, most of them king's men, they was a-shakin' in their boots."

"Outnumbered hundred to one," Salem said, "I'm thinking they can afford a little shaking."

"There wasn't but one thing we could do," Eddie whispered hoarsely.

Salem leaned in more closely, his ears pointed forward. Sabrina found herself leaning in as well. "What?" the cat asked.

"We screamed at them, to make them think we'd gone crazy."

"Screamed?" Salem repeated.

Eddie shrugged. "Usually, this can work."

Salem nodded. "Okay, you're screaming."

"Scaring them," Eddie said. He pointed two fingers at the cat's eyes. "Ye can see the fear in their eyes. They can't believe we're a-doin' this, you see."

Sabrina couldn't believe it either.

"Knowin' we got 'em fearful of us," Eddie continued, closing his right hand into a fist beside his face, "we done the one thing they couldn't have expected us to do."

"You vanished?" Salem suggested.

"Nope," Eddie said, putting his hands on either side of the cat and leaning in almost nose to nose.

34

Salem's eyes were wide pools of greenish yellow. "We charged them."

"You charged them?" Salem gasped.

Eddie nodded. "Why sure, an' it was all we could do."

"Outnumbered a hundred to one and you charged them?"

"We ran at the same end of the alley," Eddie stated, shrugging. "Figured we'd split their forces, a good and sound military tactic. Maybe we was only outnumbered fifty to one by then."

"Then what happened?" Sabrina asked, almost breathless with anticipation. The story had been going on with one hair-raising twist after another.

"We fought them!" Eddie roared in a loud voice that made Salem and Sabrina jump back. "We had at it hammer and tong, tooth and nail, I'm tellin' ye! Aye, an' why ye've never seen the likes of such a grand battle as we staged in that alley!"

"What did you do?" Salem asked.

"Why, ye great ninny," Eddie blustered, "we died! We was outnumbered fifty to one! What else was we supposed to do?" He sagged heavily onto the couch, gales of laughter thundering around the living room.

The cat's ears drooped, then flattened. He hissed angrily and leaped to the back of the couch. His yellow eyes blazed at the pirate, who was still laughing.

"A shaggy dog story?" Salem yelped. "You come in here and tell a shaggy dog story?"

Sabrina leaned back and blew a stray lock of hair

from her face in disgust. Shaggy dog stories had to be the absolute worst—especially in the hands of a master storyteller. A lot of buildup and detail went into a shaggy dog story, with absolutely no payoff in the end for the listener.

Black Eddie Peas continued roaring with laughter louder than ever when Salem stalked off and went upstairs. He slapped his knees.

"Eddie," Zelda admonished, "that was cruel."

"Oh, an' don't think I don't know it, Zellie. That was some of the best fun I've had in weeks." Laughter left the big pirate's face. "Trust me when I say it's been a long time since I've found much to laugh at."

"I never imagined you would have ever left the sea," Zelda said.

"An' I wouldna done it now, girlie, had I another choice." Eddie peered into his mug. "Blow me down, but it appears I done found the bottom of this thing again."

Zelda checked the teapot and found it was empty. "Let me brew some more."

"I'll follow ye." Eddie rose from the couch far easier than Sabrina would have believed.

"I'll get it, Eddie," Zelda offered. "You stay and rest. If there's one thing I know, it's that there isn't much rest on a pirate ship."

"I been lollygaggin' around on this couch long enough," the big pirate admitted. "Much as I hate it, it's time to get down to them troubles what brought me a-knockin' at yer door."

* * *

"Do ye remember much about King Feargus the First and the kingdom of Ootnanni?" Eddie sat on a stool near the table where Zelda kept her laptop. His heavy cutlass lay across the table before him. He idly plucked the peel from an orange.

"Of course I do." Zelda sat across from him. "We spent my whole summer as a pirate either chasing his ships or running from them."

"I don't know *anything* about King Feargus the First or Ootnanni," Sabrina spoke up. She'd quietly joined her aunts and the pirate in the kitchen, not wanting to get so much notice that they asked to be alone.

"Ootnanni is an island kingdom in the Other Realm," Zelda said. "It's in the Gentle Sea."

"Aye," Eddie said sincerely. "An' that's one sea that's been named very wrong, I guarantee ye. Ye'll find all manner of beasties and evil men a-sailin' there."

"In other words," Hilda said, "it's a perfect place to be a pirate."

Zelda and Eddie swapped looks. "Well," the pirate said, "the Gentle Sea has had her good days. Usually lots of treasure a-goin' through there. But Ootnanni has fallen on bad times."

"Before King Feargus the First took over the throne," Zelda said, "Ootnanni used to be a resort. Very touristy. You could go there, lay out on the beach, and watch a sea battle off in the distance and have dinner in the port city. A lot of witches went there, but you could find visitors from other planets and realms as well. Tres chic back then."

"Aye," Eddie said, "but that all changed when Feargus the First took over the island. He kidnapped the tourists still in Ootnanni, including a few ranking members of the Witches' Council, and ransomed them back to their families."

"It almost caused a war in the Betelgeuse system," Zelda added.

"The Witches' Council didn't do anything to stop Feargus?" Salem asked from the kitchen counter. He was living proof that the Council didn't have a sense of humor when it came to politically incorrect ideas.

"They tried," Zelda answered. "However, Feargus the First had found an ancient artifact called the Shield of the Amazing Bob that had been thought lost hundreds of years ago."

"I was told the shield was a myth," Salem protested.

"Duh," Hilda said. "I think everybody knew what you would do with it if you found it."

"Time out," Sabrina pleaded. "I'm getting mixed up between the Travel Channel and the History Channel. Who is the Amazing Bob?"

"Who was he," Zelda corrected.

"They never proved that he was dead," Hilda interrupted.

"Judging by the size of the crater left after that accident," her sister replied, "I think that's a pretty foregone conclusion."

"What about empirical evidence?" Hilda replied. "And you call yourself a scientist."

Zelda waved her sister away and focused on Sabrina. "The Amazing Bob was a warlock who had terrible control over his powers. In fact, everything he tried to do backfired on him."

"Explains the crater," Sabrina said.

"Yes. Well, Bob was attempting to create the greatest enchanted item in the history of the Witches' Council when he created the shield. By the time he finished enchanting it, no magic would work around it for miles."

"An' Ootnanni now," Eddie interjected, "is but a few miles wide itself. The Shield of the Amazing Bob covers the island plumb out into the harbors. No magic takes place in Ootnanni these days. That's why the Witches' Council has pretty much left the old reprobate alone. He may be a fierce king on the island, but once his ships go beyond the protection of the shield, they're defenseless." He shrugged. "More or less. Cap'n Cutter and us, we been makin' a right handy profit off of his ships over the years."

"You became a pirate to get the shield back," Sabrina said, looking at her aunt. "I understand now." *That makes sense.*

"Actually," Zelda said after a moment, "no. I became a pirate because I wasn't getting along with my mother that summer. She'd turned my boyfriend into a Thrallian Musklizard and lost him in the desert in one of the wilder realms. Even if I could have found him—which I didn't, though Mother later changed him back after he promised to stay away from me—I didn't have the power to undo her spell. So I became a pirate. For the summer."

"You went down to Ootnanni to become a pirate?"

"We were on a cruise ship down in that area," Zelda said. "It was simply a matter of jumping overboard and making passage on the first pirate ship that came along."

"Aye, remember it well, I do." Eddie grinned. "It was me turn up in the crow's nest, an' I seen Zellie a-floatin' out in the sea just as comfy as ye please. Cap'n Cutter gave orders to haul her aboard. Nobody knew she'd turn out to be a true pirate's pirate."

Sabrina took a deep breath. "Okay, got it. Feargus the First is the king of Ootnanni, an island where magic doesn't work. But what does he have to do with you being here?"

"King Feargus the First isn't the king of Ootnanni anymore," Eddie replied. "His son, King Feargus the Second, staged an uprisin' and locked the old king in a tower, takin' all of Ootnanni over for himself."

"How did he manage that?" Zelda asked.

Eddie sipped tea from his pewter mug. "Zellie, that boy is a right smart one, he is. Feargus the Second got rid of the old king's advisors, put his own in place, and gave his father a potion that made him addle-brained. Weren't no problem at all a-takin' over Ootnanni after that." He snorted. "If'n you thought them Ootnannians was greedy afore, you should see them landlubbers now. They'll pick a man down to his bones, then grind them bones up for fertilizer."

"I hadn't heard about that," Zelda said.

Eddie shrugged. "The Gentle Sea, Zellie, it don't cover but a small patch in all of the Other Realm. Most folk, they don't really care what goes on there."

"I know."

Sabrina thought that sounded kind of sad.

"Feargus the Second has turned out meaner than his father ever thought about," Eddie said. " 'Course, it helps that most of them no-account nobles he's got a-panderin' around the castle are greedy as this here cat." The big pirate jerked a thumb in Salem's direction.

"Hey," Salem protested, "I resent that."

Sabrina and the others ignored him.

"Ye remember the last strike we made inside Ootnanni's walls, Zellie?" Eddie asked.

"Of course. We were the first pirates to ever break into Feargus the First's treasure vaults."

Eddie smiled in fond remembrance. "Aye, an' we got off with all them gembobs and doodads that ol' King Feargus the First seemed to care so much about. Not to mention all them gold and silver coins what we spent with so much abandon."

Zelda smiled. "As I recall, King Feargus the First was pretty put out by it all. We spent the rest of the summer running from his ships."

"Aye, an' that we did. An' then some, Zellie, 'cause yer mom come and found ye at the end of that summer and took ye home. We been runnin' ever since, actually."

"Feargus the Second has been pursuing you, too?"

"Aye. With a black-hearted vengeance, I'm here to tell ye."

A concerned look filled Zelda's face. "Really? That sounds really strange."

"Strange it may be," the big pirate said, "but it's made piratin' exciting these past three hundred years. The king's navy after us, an' us a-takin' some of his cargo ships all the same. We been playin' at cat and mouse all across the Gentle Sea."

"Now that's a good game," Salem said.

Eddie grinned. "Aye, an' we made much sport of it, I promise ye. A grand game it was."

"Was?" Sabrina asked. "You're here because you lost?" Suddenly visions of the big pirate stomping around the Spellman house while he was unemployed filled her head. It wasn't a pleasant thought. Of course, after today's success at Ye Olde Doges, Black Eddie Peas might have a job really soon.

"Aye," Eddie replied bitterly. "Not just lost." He looked at Zelda. "Zellie, it's more'n that. Ye know I wouldn't a-come here if'n it was just a normal losin'. If we'd have lost the ship, why we'd have gone and fetched another. Cap'n Cutter an' us have done it afore. Ye know that."

"I do," Zelda agreed. "So what is it?"

"About twenty years ago," the big pirate said sadly, "the really bad luck started, an' it's been getting worse all the time."

"What happened?" Zelda asked.

"We was workin' hard that day, a-helpin' ourselves to the wares of an Ootnannian cargo ship a goodly distance from any of the king's navy. We was thinkin' everything was grand. See, what with all them extra ships Feargus the Second put afloat, pickins was gettin' might slim. That cargo ship was the first we'd a-taken in nearly a year." He shook his head. "That's how bad things had been, Zellie."

"Then that was a good thing," Zelda said. "You took a prize. What could be wrong with that?"

"Well, while we was a-totin' all them crates and bags aboard our ship, Ol' Agnes come up from the sea bottom. She come up between them ships so quicklike nobody saw her. Even Hawkeye Tommy didn't see her a-comin'. Next thing we know, she's a-flailin' away with them tentacles and a-snatchin' men left and right. Afore anybody can see to gettin' the ship clear, why Ol' Agnes ups and eats Cap'n Cutter like he wasn't nothin' but a tasty sea biscuit!"

☆

Chapter 4

☆

"**W**hoa!" Sabrina exclaimed, pushing back in her seat. "Gross factor and nobody warned me it was coming."

"I beg ye pardon," Eddie said politely, looking contrite. "Guess I forgot meself. Ye make yer living at sea for a lot of years, ye kind of forget what proper folks is used to."

"That's all right," Sabrina said, taking a deep breath and trying not to imagine crunching. "Ol' Agnes *ate* Captain Cutter?"

"In one big gulp." Eddie took his hat off and covered his heart for a moment.

"You never got the captain back?" Zelda asked.

"Never had the chance." Eddie put his hat back on his head and freed an orange section. He popped the orange wedge into his mouth and chewed. "Everywhere we went, why there was Feargus the Second's navy, just a-doggin' us."

44

"What did you do?" Sabrina asked.

"For a while, we cleared out of the Gentle Sea," Eddie said. "Tried our hand at cargo shipping. Of course, some of the crew, they couldn't live with us tryin' to go the straight and narrow. Just too unnatural, you know?"

"Tell me about it." Salem nodded in complete understanding. Then he looked up in surprise when everyone—including Black Eddie Peas—looked at him. "What?"

"Never mind," Hilda told the cat, shifting her attention back to the pirate. "I take it you left the cargo shipping career?"

Eddie nodded. "Left and was drove out of it. See, me and me mates put together a slick-runnin' operation. Underbid every other manjack out there lookin' to ship freight. We stayed busy. 'Course, all the other skippers and shippers hated us for it. An' then there was all them taxes and whatnot we had to pay at all the docks."

"Taxes?" Zelda asked.

"Shippin' fees and stuff like that. Warehouse rental." Eddie shook his head in exasperation. "I'm tellin' ye, Zellie, strugglin' to live life honest is just too complicated. Give me a pirate's life any day. Next thing we know, we got port authorities a-tryin' to seize our ship 'cause of unpaid taxes and dockin' fees they say we owed."

Sabrina felt bad for the pirate. Being unable to fit in was terrible.

"We escaped them," Eddie said, "then we headed

on back into the Gentle Sea. Only we run into the Ootnannian navy and got captured."

"Feargus the Second was still looking for you?"

"Aye. An' lookin' for us right hard. We come upon his ships a couple of times over the past twenty years since the Cap'n got et by Ol' Agnes, and they were still a-searchin' harder than ever for us."

"Why?" Sabrina asked.

"I'm gettin' to that," the pirate promised. "Well, during them years, Feargus the Second had gotten more cunnin' and more crafty." He lifted his shoulders and dropped them. "And, truth to tell, maybe we was somewhat desperate, too. We come up on this fat little cargo ship from Bertie's Waddle one morn and couldn't resist. You remember what Bertie's Waddle is famous for, don't you, Zellie?"

"Pastries and chocolates," Zelda answered. She looked at Sabrina, Hilda, and Salem. "Bertie's Waddle is an independent city-state along the Crescent Coast. Their desserts are absolutely to-die-for."

"With pirates in the picture," Hilda said, "I guess we can take that literally."

Zelda made a face at her.

"Aye, pastries and chocolates," Eddie replied with a smile. "An' ye know I got me a sweet tooth for them cookies they make. Anyways, we were thinkin' we were lookin' at a piece of good fortune we hadn't seen in a long time. So we swooped

46

down on the ship. Turns out that ship was a-carryin' the ammunition for the annual Crown Wars in Highhill."

"A pastry ship running guns?" Salem marveled. "Now why didn't I think of something like that?"

"They weren't a-runnin' guns," Eddie corrected. "They was a-shippin' cream pies."

"Cream pies?" Sabrina asked.

"Yes," Zelda said. "Centuries ago, Highhill kept having civil wars over who was supposed to ascend the throne. First one side would win, then the other. Both sides lost a lot of people. Finally, they agreed to stage a war with cream pies once a year for two days to figure out who was going to be king of Highhill for the next year."

"Even if we'd have been successful in a-stealin' them pies," Eddie confessed, "we'd have give them back. Bertie's Waddle would never have been able to make enough pies in time for the annual war if they'd lost that shipment."

"You weren't able to take a pastry ship?" Salem waved his paws in the air, laughing. "Boy, you guys really had gotten rusty."

Embarrassment stained Eddie's face. "The pastry ship was already taken. Feargus the Second's men decided to hold it for ransom this year, make like it was a bunch of pirates what done it. He got his ransom, too."

"But he got you and the crew as well," Zelda said.

"Aye." Eddie cleared his throat and looked at

Zelda. "We was taken in chains to Ootnanni, and we was brought before Feargus the Second. He made it plain that what he wants is the treasure what we got away with all them years ago."

"Then give it back to him," Sabrina said. "I mean, unless you spent it." *Pirate's treasure is probably a lot like allowance. Gone before you know it.*

"No way!" Salem squalled, bolting upright and flicking his tail in a frenzy. "A pirate worth his salt doesn't just *give* back a treasure he's rightfully stolen. That's booty, loot, plunder, swag, pillage, and a pirate's delight. Giving it back is just . . . just . . . *unpiratical!*"

"King Feargus the Second is holdin' some of me shipmates," Eddie said quietly. "Some of our shipmates, people you know. I don't bring that treasure back to him, he'll fit me shipmates for a hangman's noose, he will."

"Oh, Eddie, that's terrible," Zelda commented.

"You're here to see Aunt Zelda," Sabrina said, "instead of getting the treasure back to Feargus the Second. Maybe it's just me, but I'm thinking maybe there's a problem here."

"Aye, there's a problem. Ye see, we spent the gold and silver easily enough," Eddie agreed. "But it's not that he's seeking replacement of. It's them other things what we took."

"What other things?" Zelda asked. "I don't remember much of what we took."

"Don't rightly know," Eddie admitted. "Ye know how secretive the Cap'n was. Whatever was the

Cap'n's business weren't no business of yers."

"You spent the gold and silver," Sabrina said, thinking quickly, "but what happened to the rest of the treasure?"

"The Cap'n hid it, of course," Eddie stated matter-of-factly. "That's what he was forever doin' with treasures. He took a crew of mates, all of them addled by spirits, an' he went off to dig a hiding spot. Them mates what went with him, they was three sheets to the wind by the time the Cap'n settled on a place. None of them ever remembered whereat they'd been the next day. No, wherever the Cap'n hid that treasure, you can bet it's still there."

"Every good pirate hid their treasures," Salem added. "When a pirate retired, he'd need a stake to see him through his golden years."

"And pirates made treasure maps," Sabrina said excitedly. "All you have to do is find Cap'n Cutter's treasure map. Find the map, find the treasure. Easy."

"*Nobody* finds Cap'n Cutter's treasure maps," Zelda and Eddie said at the same time.

"Oh. You both seem kind of definite about that."

"We are," Zelda said.

"Actually," Eddie said, glancing at Zelda, "I was kind of hopin' ye knew where the Cap'n might have stashed the treasure this time. Ye know, on the sly?"

"I wouldn't have dreamed of doing something

like that," Zelda answered. "That would have broken Captain Cutter's first rule of piracy."

"I could have dreamed of it," Salem whispered wistfully. "And I probably will. Only now, it'll probably seem like a nightmare, digging hole after hole only to find each one empty." He cried plaintively at the thought.

"Maybe someone else on the ship knows where it is," Sabrina suggested.

"Aye, I thought of that, too. An' I asked them, but not a man aboard ship ever thought of breakin' the Cap'n's rules." Eddie glanced at Zelda shamefacedly. "I know ye give up piratin' a long time ago, Zellie. An' I know yer mom wasn't any too happy about that summer ye spent sackin' ships."

"No," Zelda agreed, "she wasn't. I was grounded for decades."

"But I'm adrift, girlie, on a treacherous sea an' no wind to fill my sails. I just remembered how the Cap'n always seemed to count on ye natural-like, and how ye always seemed to have a clever idea about things. I was just a-wonderin' if'n ye'd care enough about yer ol' shipmates to take a look into this thing with me."

"Oh, Eddie, I really don't see what kind of help I'd be."

"Well, ye can say no if'n ye want," Eddie replied, "but ye know I'd never have showed up here if'n I thought I could get out of this pickle on me own."

"Eddie," Zelda said, "I can't just—"

"Of course you can!" Salem leaped into the center of the table and addressed Zelda directly. "It's a treasure hunt! How could you not want to go?"

"Because I think the potential for me making matters worse is greater than me making matters better," Zelda replied. "I was never a real pirate."

"Oh, ye may say that, Zellie," Eddie told her enthusiastically, "but ye are a natural, if'n I'm any judge—an' I am. What we need here is a dose of them clever wits ye always carry around with yerself."

"But I don't know where the treasure is, Eddie."

"We can *find* it, girlie. Together, I know we can. An' if we don't, all them fine men ye served with are gonna be dancin' on air in a few days, victims of ol' Jack Ketch."

Sabrina saw the worried look on her aunt's face and knew the thought didn't set well with her.

"I'm good at treasure hunts," Salem exclaimed. "Maybe you don't know it, but I've got a nose for treasure."

"Salem," Hilda interrupted, "you can't even find the cat treats we hide from you in this house."

"That's not treasure," the cat protested.

"The way you act," Hilda retorted, "you couldn't tell it."

"Look," Salem said desperately, "we have to do this. It's a good deed, right? How can you turn down a good deed, a cry for help, a plea for succor? Eddie's your friend, Zelda."

"He did help Harvey at the mall," Sabrina pointed out.

"This really doesn't sound like a good idea." Zelda frowned, but Sabrina could tell it was her aunt's giving-in frown, the one that was more for show than anything else. "Maybe I could do something."

"Aye," Eddie cheered. "Now that's the spirit!" He looked at Sabrina. "An' ye should come too, lass. Seein' the sights, breathin' the ocean air, I'm thinkin' ye'd find it right agreeable."

For a moment, Sabrina played with the idea of going along. Visions of ocean waves and beaches filled her head. *And shopping! I bet I could find some really good bargains!* The Other Realm could always be counted on for really cool stuff. Of course, not all of it could be brought back to the mortal realm, and sometimes her aunts did say no. *After Eddie arrived, I really didn't get to do any of the shopping I'd planned.* Part of her really, really wanted to go.

"Can't," she replied. "I've got a date with Harvey tonight." Dating Harvey was the best thing.

"Ah, lass," Eddie said, "ye really don't know what yer a-missin'."

"Take pictures," Sabrina suggested. "You can tell me all about it after you get the treasure and save the crew."

The doorbell rang.

"I'll get it." Sabrina got up from the table and

walked into the living room. When she opened the door, she found Mr. Kraft standing there. His jacket was still stained with ketchup.

"I'd like to see Zelda if she has a moment," the principal said with tight politeness.

"Sure," Sabrina said. "Come on in." She waved him to a chair and turned to find Zelda coming from the kitchen with Black Eddie Peas at her heels. The pirate had to duck under the doorway.

"I'll make a list of things we'll need," Zelda was saying, lost in thought, not noticing that Mr. Kraft was there. "Equipment, supplies, maps. How are the cannon? We're going to have to have cannon if we're going to—"

"Aunt Zelda," Sabrina said loudly, watching Mr. Kraft's face. The principal glared at the pirate and seemed to be confused by Zelda's conversation. "Look who's here to see you."

Zelda looked up reluctantly. The reluctance quickly gave way to shock, then concern. "Willard. You're here. *Why* are you here?"

"After this morning's debacle," Mr. Kraft said, "I wanted to check on you." He stared at Eddie with strong displeasure.

"I'm fine," Zelda said, still trying to recover. "How are you?"

"Quite frankly, Zelda, I've been better. The police reports took much more time to fill out, were unnecessarily personal, and turned out to be a complete waste of time. Gerry's father bought off a judge or something."

"I doubt he'd do something like that."

"The charges were dropped in less than five minutes. Something like that would never happen in my school. The guilty parties would be punished no matter who their fathers were."

"I know. I'm sorry you had to go through that."

Mr. Kraft stared at Black Eddie Peas. "One word of caution, though. It seems the police might be interested in talking to your cousin."

"I thought we'd worked that all out at the mall."

Mr. Kraft pushed his glasses back up on his nose with his forefinger. "I'm just saying it's a possibility. If he has some kind of record, things could go hard on him. I don't think Attorney Naylor was any too pleased about how his son was treated."

"The boy's lucky I didn't tear him limb from limb," Eddie growled. "I'd have had him walk the plank and fed him to the fishes if it'd been me."

Mr. Kraft blinked owlishly at the pirate, and Sabrina almost lost it.

"I'm sure," Mr. Kraft said slowly, "that wouldn't have been acceptable. Really sure."

Eddie flopped back down on the couch, taking up all the available space. "An' don't you worry your head about me an' them king's men. I've been getting around the law and them what uphold it since I was just a lad."

Mr. Kraft smiled uncomfortably. "Somehow, that doesn't surprise me at all."

" 'Tis a gift," Eddie confided.

"I'm glad to see you, Willard," Zelda said, "but I'm afraid you've come at a bad time."

"I have?"

"Yes. I've got to take my cousin to the airport. I hope you understand."

"Sure, sure. I know how it is with unexpected company. They arrive in town, cause a commotion, then you have to get them out of town before the police catch up to them."

"It's not like that, Willard."

"I'm just kidding." Mr. Kraft gave a big grin to show that he was kidding.

He's not kidding, Sabrina thought.

"Well, I guess I'll be going," Mr. Kraft said. "Just wanted to check in on you."

"Thank you," Zelda said.

"However," the principal went on, "the remark about the cannon you made earlier intrigues me. You did mention a cannon, didn't you? I mean, I might have heard you wrong."

"Not a cannon," Eddie said gruffly. "Zellie was talking about *cannon,* a great bloody lot of them, to fill the air with grapeshot and exploding shells."

"Lovely," Mr. Kraft said.

Sabrina headed up the stairs to her room, knowing her aunt was doomed to a long explanation, for once the principal had gotten interested he was hard to dissuade.

"It's for a War of Independence reenactment," Zelda said.

"With pirates?" Mr. Kraft asked.

"Cousin Eddie is sailing with Jean Lafitte's navy down in New Orleans."

Sabrina closed the door behind her.

Things are really desperate, Sabrina thought as she looked through the selection of clothing in her closet. *How can I not find anything to wear?* But she couldn't. Nothing seemed really special enough. After the hard day Harvey had gone through at Ye Olde Doges, she really wanted something . . . something . . .

She sighed; she didn't even know what she wanted. *Not a good sign.* She walked over to the full-length mirror in her room and started pointing up outfits. She tried a midnight blue mini, but knew instantly that Harvey would be intimidated because it was so dressy. He'd be tired and worn out, wanting to relax.

She pointed again, clothing herself in a turquoise V-neck pucker T-shirt and khaki low cargo flares. *Okay! Maybe we're getting somewhere.* She pointed up a pair of Skechers sneakers.

"I can't believe you're picking pizza over plunder," Salem grumped from where he lay on the bed.

Sabrina ignored the cat. *Now let's do something about that hair.*

"You can't believe what it's like," the cat groused. "You're out there on the seas, rolling between the waves with a full spread of sailcloth laid on, way out of sight of land, and you're pulling up someone else's treasure."

"Maybe that's your idea of a great evening, but it's not mine." Sabrina pointed her hair into a ponytail, then decided she didn't like it.

"Get a little treasure in your hands," Salem suggested. "You'll change your tune."

"No, I won't. I have my priorities right, thank you very much."

"Sometimes," the cat sighed, "you can be a real stick-in-the-mud."

"Better than being a chew toy for Ol' Agnes."

"Ol' Agnes is a myth," Salem protested. "No one has ever seen her."

"Eddie said he did."

"Are you going to believe everything he tells you?"

"No." Sabrina pointed barrettes into her hair along with a neat part. *Better, but not there yet.* "But he was the one who mentioned the treasure."

"Pirates never lie about treasure."

"What about the shaggy dog story?"

"That was just a story."

"Uh-huh." Sabrina pointed her hair to hang loose and natural, then added a headband. *Now* that *I like.*

"If we were there, we could cut ourselves in for a share."

"Splitting the treasure isn't going to help Eddie's friends."

Salem snorted. "Eddie's friends need to look out for themselves."

The phone rang before Sabrina could reply. She

calmed herself, let out a sigh, and told herself she wasn't going to argue with the cat. "Hello," she said, cradling the handset to her ear.

"Sab? It's Harvey." He sounded hesitant and down, very un-Harveyish. "I've got some bad news."

Sabrina's heart pounded. "Are you all right?"

Chapter 5

"**M**y relief called in and quit," Harvey said. "I'm kind of stuck here at the stand."

"For how long?" Sabrina asked, calming down. Harvey was okay; that was all that mattered.

"Probably till the mall closes."

"Can't they get someone else?"

"They're trying," Harvey replied, "but my boss told me it really wasn't looking good. The people who work the stand during the week haven't had a day off in a long time and he couldn't get in touch with them."

Sabrina tried to look on the good side. "That's okay. The mall closes at nine. We could skip the movie and still have pizza."

"Not really. After all the business today, there's a lot of cleanup and restocking left to do tonight. I don't think I'm going to make it out of here before

59

eleven. And I'm pulling a really long shift. I'm bushed. Sorry, Sab."

Sabrina felt bad. She didn't even think about all the work Harvey had been doing. "I'm sorry, Harvey. You must be worn out."

Harvey sighed. "This is worse than two-a-day practices for football."

"Maybe we can catch a matinee tomorrow," Sabrina suggested.

"That sounds cool." A conversation sounded in the background, and Harvey told someone he would be right there. "Hey, I gotta go."

"Sure."

"I know you're disappointed, Sab, but I'll make it up to you."

"It's okay. Really." *It was so not okay.* Harvey's sense of responsibility was another thing she liked about him. It was just kind of hard adjusting to the fact that he was responsible to more than just her.

"Thanks for understanding, Sab. You're the best." Harvey said good-bye quickly and hung up the phone.

"He cancelled out on you?" Salem asked as Sabrina cradled the phone.

"Yes." Sabrina looked at her reflection in the mirror. *All dressed up and no place to go. Bummer!*

"Well," Salem said, "you can hang around the house and mope in pajamas and bunny slippers, munching on a quart of Rocky Road ice cream, or—"

"Or?" Sabrina prompted.

"Or," Salem said, wagging his tail slowly the way

he did when he occasionally stalked mice he made sure he never caught, "you can do something else."

"Like what?"

"I was thinking exotically. You, me, a beach at sunset. You with a shovel, me with a pail, the pleasant thump of that shovel striking a buried treasure chest." The cat sighed dreamily, his eyes winking satisfaction.

"That treasure's not yours."

"It could be. With a little effort, and maybe just a smidgen of help."

"Aunt Zelda will never let you go."

"She will if you do," Salem said. "I'm your familiar. What kind of witch would you be if you ran off and left your familiar behind?"

"Oh," Sabrina said, "*happy* comes to mind. So do *relieved*, *secure*, and *worry-free*."

"If I had a human face," the cat chided, "it would be frowning now."

Sabrina pointed herself into pj's and pink bunny slippers. She looked at her slippers. The bunny ears drooped sadly. *Getting ready for bed before seven o'clock? No way.* She crossed to her bedroom doorway and saw Hilda coming up the stairs. "Good. You guys haven't left yet."

"No, there are a few things I need to get." Excitement shone in Hilda's eyes. "I haven't been to a pirate den in a long time. I'm looking forward to this."

"Mind some company? Harvey's stuck working at Ye Olde Doges, so the date's off."

"Sure. It'll be fun," Hilda said, continuing to her

room. "Except for that whole find-the-treasure-and-save-the-pirates-from-the-gallows thing."

"And Ol' Agnes," Zelda said, coming up the steps. "A crotchety sea monster is never fun. So you're coming?"

"Yes." Sabrina pointed at her pj's and bunny slippers, changing them into buccaneer pants, rolled-top boots, and a long-sleeved blouse that she judged to be properly piratical. A scarlet scarf bound her golden locks, and a patch covered one eye. She hoisted a cutlass with as much enthusiasm as she could muster. "I guess it's a pirate's life for me!"

"This is the Gentle Sea?" Sabrina stared at the rolling wall of water coming toward them. Another wave followed it, then another, staggering back endlessly till they dropped out of sight over the curve of the horizon.

"Aye," Black Eddie Peas answered, a lopsided grin on his bearded face. "An' I tole ye it was named wrong, now didn't I?"

"Yeah," Sabrina replied, "but I didn't think it was named this wrong." She stood on the docks, where they'd appeared after entering the linen closet back in the Spellman house. They hadn't been able to appear at their real destination due to the magic-disrupting effects of the Shield of the Amazing Bob.

The Gentle Sea rolled out farther than her eyes could see. The rising curve of five-foot-tall white-capped gray-green waves curled into the shoreline, smacking loudly against the dock pilings—the tall, thick timbers the docks were built on. Seagulls littered the irregular and uneven wooden docks that lined the piers. Over two dozen ships occupied the harbor, sitting at anchor while crews worked to unload the cargo. Rigging slapped against the masts, making them sound hollow. Men's voices raised in friendship and in frustration carried across the water.

"I smell fish," Salem said, sticking his head up from where Sabrina carried him in her arms.

"How could you not?" Sabrina wrinkled her nose. The smell was stronger than she remembered from past visits to beaches. However, the other beaches she'd visited lately hadn't had wagons of ice covered with tuna, cod, and lobsters.

"Excuse me," Zelda said to a passing sailor. "Could you help me find *Bright Racer?*"

The old sailor squinted up from beneath shaggy iron gray brows. "Didn't know it was lost."

"It's not lost," Zelda said. "I'm lost."

"Get shanghaied, did ye?" the sailor asked. "I've had that happen a few times. We'll, ye're in Smythport. Have ye heard of it?"

Eddie stepped forward. "Why, ye lily-livered nincompoop, of course we've heard of Smythport. We're here, ain't we?"

The old sailor frowned. "I wasn't the one what said ye was lost." He pointed at Zelda. "It was she."

"Eddie," Zelda said, "let me handle this."

The big pirate scowled and stepped back.

"I didn't make myself clear," Zelda said. "We're looking for *Bright Racer.*"

"Whyn't ye say so?" the sailor demanded sourly. He hooked a thumb over his bony shoulder. *"Bright Racer*'s down six ships. Can't miss her. If'n ye don't mind, what are ye a-lookin' for that ship for? Cap'n Quirk owe ye money?"

Zelda shook her head. "No. We're booking passage to Governor's Island."

The old sailor's face wrinkled. "On *Bright Racer?*"

Zelda nodded. "We were told it was the only ship departing for Governor's Island now."

"Well, that's probably right," the old sailor admitted. "But afore I'd trust meself to *Bright Racer,* I think I'd just tie an anchor around me neck and jump into the deepest part of the Gentle Sea. Save ye some time, by gum!" He moved on, heading for one of the many taverns lining the dock.

"That didn't sound very positive," Sabrina said. She followed Zelda and Eddie, her eyes drinking in all the sights around her. Besides the wagons filled with ice and fish, there were carts containing clothing, fruit, cheeses, cages of chickens, goats, and vegetables. Women and children called out to her, offering samples of their wares.

Planks led from the docks to the ships. Huge cargo nets held crates and bundles suspended from a great boom arm. The bundles settled on the decks and docks with great thumps that sent vibrations through the boardwalk Sabrina walked on.

Most of the people and the sailors wore homespun clothing that had seen better days. Their faces were haggard and drawn, and most of them didn't seem happy. There were more frowns than smiles. That bothered Sabrina a lot.

"This isn't the idyllic Caribbean getaway I'd imagined," she said. "This is actually kind of depressing. I thought there'd be parties."

"No parties here, girlie," Eddie stated quietly, his eyes roving over their surroundings. His hand never moved far from the cutlass. "Betwixt the greed of their rulers, these people are havin' a hard go of it. I can remember when there were happy days here, though. Was hardly a time that ye walked along Smythport without hearin' 'a somebody a-singin'. An' then it didn't take much more than the sun a-risin'."

"I remember," Zelda said sadly. "Oh, Eddie, this is terrible."

"I know, Zellie. I hated a-comin' to get ye, because I know how much ye loved that summer ye spent here. I didn't want to take them memories away from ye. Folks around here have fallen on bad times."

Five ships down, they found *Bright Racer.* Sabrina knew it was the right ship because the name had been painted under the crossed-out name *Jaunty.* But she couldn't believe the ship.

Bright Racer held three masts located fore, aft, and amidships. The sails were furled around the masts, but they looked almost black with ground-in dirt and mold. The cargo ship floated listlessly at anchor, heeling over to the left a little. A half-dozen men stood and sat around the cargo hold. It had been years since the ship had been near a coat of paint.

"Oh my," Zelda said, shocked.

Salem pushed up from Sabrina's arms and stared at the ship in consternation. "We're all going to die."

"I'm not going to be sick, I'm not going to be sick," Sabrina chanted as she felt the deck shifting beneath her feet. She stood in *Bright Racer*'s prow, the wind whipping her hair. Her stomach rolled again. *I gave up comfortable pj's, television, and a quart of Rocky Road ice cream to come here. Stupid, stupid, stupid!*

"I'm not going to die, I'm not going to die," Salem whimpered beside her.

"You know," Hilda said from behind them, "it's going to get much worse when we actually get under way."

Sabrina's stomach rebelled at the thought. So far they were still at anchorage at Smythport. "I know. When are we leaving?"

"Soon, I think. Captain Quirk is finishing his 'negotiations' with the port authority." Hilda nodded at the docks.

Sabrina watched as the captain handed a small bag of gold coins to one of the men dressed in the purple port authority uniforms. The uniformed man opened the bag, spilled the coins into his hand, and counted them. Captain Quirk protested, but none of the guards paid any attention to him.

Satisfied with the bag's contents, the port authority guard walked to the water's edge and peered down. "Hey, Cecil!" he yelled.

Sabrina glanced down as well. Shadows shifted in front of the cargo ship beneath the rolling waves. Then a massive serpent's head pushed up.

The serpent's tongue flicked out repeatedly. It blinked its eyes and focused on Salem. "Sssssnack," it hissed. An excited grin split its lipless mouth. "Hello, Sssssnack."

Salem froze. "I'm going to be a monster munchie." Then he exploded into action, digging his claws into the railing and hurling himself behind Sabrina. He pressed tightly against the back of her legs.

In disbelief, Sabrina watched the serpent's head swing toward her, dripping seawater. It turned its head only an arm's length away from her so it could focus one cold, black eye on her.

"Not ssssnack," the sea serpent intoned sadly.

"That's right," Sabrina said, her voice quavering. Her legs refused to move; they felt like they'd been nailed to the deck. The mouth looked big enough to swallow her in one long gulp. "Not snack."

The sea serpent nodded happily, suddenly focusing on Sabrina. "Not ssssnack, ssssupper!"

"Eeep!" Sabrina squeaked.

"Yo, Cecil!" the port authority guard shouted.

Reluctantly, the sea serpent turned toward the man on the docks.

"Their bill's been paid in full," the port authority guard said. "Let them go."

"Ssssure," Cecil said. "First, ssssnack."

The port authority guard signaled for a group of men to approach the sea serpent with a half-dozen wicker baskets of fish. They upended the baskets and poured the fish into the creature's gaping maw. Cecil made short work of the fish, smacking contentedly.

"Now let them go," the port authority guard called out when the last of the fish was gone.

"Of coursssse," the sea serpent agreed. Shadows shifted in the shallows of the harbor, uncoiling from the cargo ship.

Bright Racer rocked and bobbed on the waves even more, making Sabrina hang on to the railing. Her stomach spasmed.

"Any more work?" the sea serpent asked.

"Not yet," the port authority guard replied. "We'll call you when we need you again."

"Csssertainly. Thankssss." Quietly, the sea serpent eased beneath the water and disappeared, swimming for the deeper reaches of the Gentle Sea.

"A sea serpent ship boot?" Sabrina asked.

"Evidently it works," Hilda replied.

Sabrina shook her head. "This is totally weird."

"Not too weird yet, girlie," Eddie assured her. "Ye ain't met Ol' Agnes yet."

After *Bright Racer* got under way, Sabrina's seasickness actually got better. She stood in the prow, listening to the wind crack the big sails above her. She held tightly to the small ropes that held the sails and poles in place. Black Eddie Peas had told her that the small ropes were called ratlines and the poles supporting the sails were called yardarms and rigging. She tried to think of them that way, but it was all still alien.

She stared out at the sea. The sun, paler than normal, hung in front of them in the cerulean blue sky. The ship rode up the incoming waves, the deck tilting steeply, then it crashed through the white-capped roller at the top. Now that she'd gotten used to the movement, it was almost like being on an amusement park ride.

Eddie stood beside her, not holding on to the ratlines, his body adjusting naturally to the rise and fall of the ship. She knew that his thoughts were somber, a long way from them.

"Why do they call this ship *Bright Racer* instead of 'the' *Bright Racer?*" Sabrina asked.

"On account of it's the ship's name," Eddie said, glancing at her. He seemed glad of the distraction. "It would be like a-callin' ye 'the' Sabrina. Wouldn't make much sense, now would it?"

"No, I guess not." Sabrina was quiet for a moment. "So what made you become a pirate?"

"Oh, girlie, I didn't set out to become a pirate." Eddie grinned. "It was the sea what pulled me in. More'n anythin', I wanted to sail, to be out here on it like this." He took a deep breath. "To me way of thinkin', there ain't no finer place. I started out as a sailor when I come of age. Crewed aboard a merchanter, a-ferryin' goods and people back and forth.

But it was too much of the same, an' not nearly excitin' enough. One day I was shanghaied by Cap'n Cutter, and the rest is history."

Bright Racer sailed up another tall wall of water. Out on the open Gentle Sea, the swells were coming ten and twelve feet high. Dark purple clouds gathered in the sky overhead, threatening rain. Another wave came right after the last, catching the cargo ship and actually pushing it back for a moment. Then the wind filled the sails again and drove them forward.

Sabrina kept her fingers knotted up in the ratlines. *It would be so much easier to magic the sea quieter or just fly the boat over,* she thought. But Aunt Zelda had been adamant about not using magic. This far into the magic-free zone created by the Shield of the Amazing Bob, Zelda didn't want anyone using magic.

As the cargo ship started down the back side of the wave, a reptilian shape formed in the nearby water. The monstrous creature looked like a crocodile, but from snout to tail it was longer than *Bright Racer.* It swam on top of the ocean for a moment, one rolling eye fixed on the cargo ship. Then its huge tail whipped the water, and it disappeared again.

"Did you see that?" Sabrina croaked.

"Aye," Eddie said, somewhat pale. "An' how could ye miss a thing such as that? It was a right big ripper."

"A ripper?" Sabrina laughed despite the fear that

filled her. "You're familiar with *The Croc Hunter?*" *The Croc Hunter* was a show that ran on the Discovery Channel, and it was one of Harvey's favorite shows.

"Me and the crew," Eddie said, "we usually caught the show in Slimy Virgil's back in Wheatstone, one of the port cities we worked out of during our cargo-hauling days. Some of the other port cities get the cable channels. Illegally, of course. Just one more act of piracy in a day's business."

Sabrina gazed out at the rolling sea again, noting the terns following along in the cargo ship's wake. "The Gentle Sea really is filled with monsters, isn't it?"

The pirate hesitated for a moment, then looked away from her. "Aye. I won't lie to ye, girlie. This thing I asked yer aunt to do, why it's a dangerous thing. We see to it bein' done all properlike, we're a-gonna be facing some of them sea beasties. Most likely, we'll cross courses with Ol' Agnes her own self."

"The story you told," Sabrina asked, "about Old Agnes eating Captain Cutter? That was true, wasn't it?"

"Aye. Seen her, meself. That day, I could have reached out and touched her. Maybe if I'd acted faster, I could have saved the Cap'n."

"What can you tell me about her?"

Eddie shrugged. "Ol' Agnes, some say, has been in the Gentle Sea since it were first a puddle. Very few have ever seen her, but plenty have felt her wrath. She's a night-feeder most times. Likes to come upon a ship in the darkness, wrap her tentacles around it, then drag down the vessel and all hands on her."

Despite the balmy air, Sabrina shivered, thinking about the giant crocodile.

"Some," Eddie went on, "says that Ol' Agnes is the empress of the Gentle Sea. They tell stories that she can control any creature that swims through or flies above these waters."

Salem blew a raspberry.

"Do you believe that?" Sabrina asked, ignoring the cat's rude behavior.

"I ain't rightly certain, girlie. I've heard a lot of things I thought couldn't be true but were, but there's just too much to know for sure. Me, I'm a-thinkin' that aye, it is true."

"Give me a break," Salem said. "Ol' Agnes is an old wives' tale if anything. A nightmare left over from a late-night anchovy pizza binge. Those can be terrible. I mean, c'mon. One monster out ruling all the others? She's a myth, a folk tale used to scare children and superstitious pirates."

Eddie shoved his hard face next to the cat's, almost nose to nose. "Ye only says that so high and mighty-like, whiskers, 'cause ye never once looked into Ol Agnes's big, ugly eye for yerself."

"Yeah?" Salem replied, flattening his ears.

"Aye," Eddie growled.

Cat and pirate bristled at each other. Without warning, *Bright Racer* smashed through another wave. This time a wall of water splashed over the railing. Sabrina quickly got out of the way and watched as the seawater drenched Eddie and Salem. Angry cat hisses and curses filled the air.

"Land ho!" the young sailor above them in the crow's nest suddenly yelled out.

Chapter 6

☆

"*G*overnor's Island," Black Eddie Peas whispered, abandoning his argument with Salem. He walked over to join Sabrina at the ship's prow and peered out at the fogbound land. His face held a trace of fear and doubt. "Once we get in there, we're a-gonna know we're in for it for sure."

Sabrina took out the small brass spyglass she'd pointed up with her outfit, extended it, and fitted it to her eye.

In the distance, a rugged coastline flecked with patchy gray fog stood out against the Gentle Sea. Mountains started almost immediately behind the bowl-shaped beach, stretching up into low-lying clouds. The wood and stone houses stood close together, looking like a child's blocks. Docks lined with ships and sailors covered the beach.

The harbor was shaped like an elongated crescent moon. The points of the rocky land came so close to each other that Sabrina guessed no more than five or six ships at a time could enter the big harbor. Two stone towers occupied the ends of the crescent. Uniformed guards stood inside the tower rooms. A chain-link gate hung between the two towers, barring entrance or exit to the harbor. High stone walls had been built from the towers that led back to the port city.

"That there is Governor's Town," Eddie said. "They keep it guarded at all times. Once we get in, there's no promise that we're getting out again."

That, Sabrina thought, *doesn't sound good.*

"Ahoy, *Bright Racer!* By the power granted by His Magnificence Governor Leroy, governor of Governor's Island, and in the name of Queen Becca, herself ruler of the Foggy Isle Kingdom, I tell you to state your business and declare your cargo."

Sabrina thought the guardsman on the Governor's Patrol sounded a little bored, but there was no mistaking the dozens of crossbows aimed at the cargo ship from the two guard towers. She swallowed hard, suddenly realizing the trip wasn't nearly as carefree as she'd thought it would be. *Why am I always getting this when it's too late?*

"Hidey-ho," Captain Quirk called out jovially from the amidships railing. He was a short man, but incredibly fat. Rings decorated his fingers, and gold chains hung around his neck. His beard was carefully trimmed and kept short. "We're the good ship

Bright Racer, hailing from Smythport with cargo and passengers."

"Stand by to be boarded. I'm Commander Kelvin." The guardsman waved his boat crew into action. The crew dug oars into the water and propelled the small skiff from the guard tower dock to the cargo ship.

Quirk smiled graciously and ordered his crew to toss the rope ladder over the side.

Sabrina felt nervous. The cargo ship had dropped her sails and sat bobbing on the water next to the chain-link gate. The tinny screeching of the links against *Bright Racer*'s hull echoed around her.

The patrol members on the tower above and on the tower at the other end of the gate kept their weapons at the ready. Commander Kelvin climbed the rope ladder quickly, followed by his men.

"I'm really thinking now that I shouldn't have allowed you to come, Sabrina." Zelda watched the Governor's Patrol guards uncomfortably as they began their inspection of the cargo ship.

"Well," Sabrina said, "we crossed the Gentle Sea without seeing Old Agnes. That's got to be a good sign."

Commander Kelvin opened the scrolls Quirk gave him, reading over the lists of goods the cargo ship carried. But the commander also kept his eyes on Black Eddie Peas.

"Actually, it might have been better if we had run into Old Agnes," Zelda said. "I'm going to need to talk to her."

"Talk to a sea monster?" Sabrina yelped. "No way."

"She has Captain Cutter," Zelda insisted.

"Ewwww." Sabrina wrinkled her nose in disgust. "Old Agnes ate him, and whatever's left of him after all these years is something I'm pretty sure you don't want."

"Everybody who knows the truth about Old Agnes knows she never eats anyone. She just swallows them and keeps them captive."

"For twenty years?"

"Ol' Agnes," Eddie spoke up, "that's one likes to play with her food afore she finishes it off." He paused. "That's kind of what Governor Leroy does with all them prisoners down in the dungeons."

"Dungeons?" Sabrina looked through the chain-link gate at the port town waiting on the other side. "Nobody said anything about dungeons. Dungeons aren't a good thing when your powers aren't working." She'd noticed that her finger had felt sprained earlier when she'd tried to point up a bottle of flavored water.

"Aye." Eddie rubbed his bearded chin restlessly. "The dungeons are down in the catacombs beneath the Governor's Mansion. The governor's torturers are renowned for their evil skills."

"That's probably one of the things that put this little hot spot on the map," Salem commented sarcastically. "Come visit the Gentle Sea and feed the sea monsters. Visit Governor's Island and get drawn and quartered. Terrific."

Eddie grinned at the cat. "What happened to all those dreams about finding treasure?"

"Those are the only things keeping me aboard ship," Salem replied. He looked out at the sea. "That, and all this water."

"Look out!" a crewman yelled. Immediately, everyone on *Bright Racer*'s deck took cover, including the Governor's Patrol members. The cargo ship rolled over to starboard as a massive shape suddenly surfaced nearby.

An incredibly long, slender neck propelled a wedge-shaped head nearly four feet across high into the air. The long jaws popped open to reveal dozens of serrated teeth. Gray hide mottled with aquamarine splotches looked tough as leather.

Narrowly missing, the creature snapped at a white seagull that was flying low over the ocean to capture bits of food. Feathers flew, drifting along in the mild breeze. The seagull shrilled in alarm and sped away too quickly for the huge creature to follow.

Sabrina saw the monster's huge body floating in the water beside *Bright Racer*. The creature was nearly all head and neck, but the long, triangular flippers looked strong and wicked. The big head turned, swinging at the end of the long neck, and hard yellow eyes regarded the cargo ship crew and their guests.

"That's an elasmosaurus," Zelda informed them in quiet wonderment. "It's from the plesiosaur family. They're believed to be extinct in the mortal realm."

The gigantic monster came closer to the ship.

Water dripped from its open maw onto the deck. Sabrina didn't think anyone was breathing; she knew she wasn't.

"It won't eat us," Eddie reassured them. "We're too big for it to get into its gullet." He drew his cutlass and walked toward the elasmosaurus. He yelled and waved his weapon.

The monster regarded the pirate curiously, coming closer.

"Now's probably not the time to bring this up," Sabrina said, "but what if that thing isn't just a gulper? You know, maybe it's actually a closet nibbler."

Eddie continued yelling and waving. The elasmosaurus curled its lips back, twisting its head from side to side. Suddenly it darted forward again, reaching past the pirate, snaking across the deck and streaking for Salem.

Reacting quickly, Sabrina grabbed a mop from a nearby pail. Captain Quirk wasn't a neat freak by any stretch of the imagination. The water in the mop pail reeked with a soured brine odor that Sabrina felt certain was responsible for peeling some of the ship's paint.

Sabrina slapped the sea monster in the face with the drenched mop, and the sour stink spread everywhere. "No!" she yelled. "You're not getting my cat!"

Salem scampered out of the way, and the elasmosaurus's head thumped against the deck almost hard enough to jar the teen witch from her feet. The nasty mop head got stuck in one of the sea monster's flaring nostrils.

"Oh, now *that's* gotta hurt," Salem observed from Sabrina's feet.

A quiver ran the length of the creature's neck as it shook its head, trying desperately to dislodge the mop trapped in its nose. It honked in terror and withdrew from the cargo ship, pushing hard against the hull. *Bright Racer* rolled to the side deeply enough to take on water from an incoming wave.

Sabrina lost her footing and fell. She slid across the deck toward the railing, certain she was going to go over the side. *Know what sea monsters call people who fall into the sea?* she thought before she could stop herself. *Croutons!* Just before she went over the railing, Eddie grabbed her wrist.

"Hold on, girlie!" the pirate shouted, saving her from going over. "I've got ye!"

In the next moment, the cargo ship righted, throwing everyone to the other side. Then it rolled back again. Sabrina slid around the deck, unable to get her balance. The ship bobbed back and forth another half-dozen times. During that whole time, Captain Quirk and his crew seemed to deal with the back-and-forth motion of the ship with relative ease. *Bright Racer*'s crew grabbed on to things, rode out the rough ride, then went stumbling back across to the other side of the cargo ship in sync.

Wow, Sabrina thought. *They must go through this a lot.*

When the ship finally leveled out better, the elasmosaurus was nowhere to be seen. Sabrina stood near the railing on shaking legs. "I can't believe I did that."

Eddie smiled at her, his eyes twinkling. "Ah, girlie, ye did yerself well, ye did. Why yer aunt back in her day was just as feisty as ye are."

Aunt Zelda? Sabrina looked at her aunt in disbelief. Zelda was always the calm, rational one.

"Did you see that?" Salem clung worriedly to the railing, looking out into the gray-green sea where the elasmosaurus had disappeared. "That thing tried to eat me."

"Don't take it so hard, whiskers," Eddie said. "Why them things, if ye cook them just right, they taste just like chicken."

"Chicken sounds good," Salem said. "And something that big, there would be plenty."

Eddie roared with laughter, and Sabrina noticed that the sound seemed to make the governor's guards nervous. She supposed they were used to everyone being afraid of them.

"I don't think ye'll be a-seein' that partic'lar beastie again," Eddie said. "He knows if'n he comes around here a-showin' his ugly face again, why Sabrina would just mop the place up with him all over again!" He clapped her on the back. "Wouldn't ye, girlie?"

"Sure." Sabrina smiled weakly. *I never want to see anything else like that again.* Then another thought filled her head. "That thing was pretty big. Was it bigger than Old Agnes?"

Eddie grew more serious. "No. That thing, why it rocked this old tub easy enough, but Ol' Agnes, she could have dragged this ship under—and us with it."

"Oh." Sabrina glanced at Zelda. "And I suppose there's no getting around talking to Old Agnes?"

Zelda shook her head. "I'm afraid not."

Terrific, Sabrina thought. The makeup date with Harvey on Sunday seemed even further away than ever.

"Wow, this place is like one big spring break party town." Sabrina gazed in delighted wonder at the men and women who filled the dirt road leading up from the harbor.

The town's residents and visitors stood in front of wood and stone shops and taverns. Hand-scrawled and professionally made signs warred for attention, advertising a leather goods store, a blacksmith's shop, several taverns, hostels, fortune-tellers, sail-cloth-makers, carpenters, masons, candle makers, and dozens of other trade and goods shops.

People haggled with vendors selling fruit and chickens from carts parked in the alleys between the small buildings. Jugglers and mimes entertained the thronging crowds for coins tossed into small wooden boxes. Balladeers, musicians, and dancers occupied storefronts, standing on small stages, in the backs of carts, or on small crates.

Sabrina followed Eddie and Zelda through the crowds. Everybody seemed to give way automatically before the big pirate. People bumped into Sabrina repeatedly, none of them offering apologies, too carried away by the festival around them.

"Hey, hey, hey," Salem grumped after a large lady charged into them and almost knocked Sabrina down. Sabrina was carrying Salem in a backpack, an agreement they'd made when they'd docked at the harbor and the cat had whined until she'd given in. "We're walking here, we're walking here."

The large woman's attention seemed riveted on Black Eddie Peas. But at Salem's words, she turned around and shook a fist at him. "You don't be rude, cat, else Jasmine reach down your t'roat and rip out your tongue."

Sabrina hurried on and Jasmine ignored them. Only a little farther ahead, the crowd's attention was drawn upward.

Two stories above, a young man walked a tightrope tied to buildings on opposite sides of the street. He carried a pink and purple parasol with colorful fishes dangling from strings. The young man teetered uncertainly, waving his arms and the parasol, looking frightened. The crowd *oohed* and *ahhed* in appreciation and concern.

"What is Tommy doing up there?" Zelda asked.

Eddie grinned and shrugged. "Ye know Tommy, Zellie. That boy can't stand to be bored none."

"Tommy?" Sabrina asked. "You know him?"

Above, the tightrope walker balanced precariously on one foot, waving comically. For a long moment it looked like he was going to fall, his other foot high in the air as he flailed backward.

Then he recovered, bowed in the center of the rope, and the audience clapped loudly in appreciation.

"That's Tommy Hawkeyes," Eddie said proudly. "He's the best ye'll ever find in the upper rigging of a ship. Sharp eyes, too."

"He could fall and break his neck," Sabrina said.

The young daredevil continued his trek to the other end of the rope, making it sway several inches as he balanced precariously above it.

"Not if'n he don't," Eddie said.

Sabrina continued watching, suddenly realizing the young pirate didn't look any older than Harvey. She stepped up beside Zelda. "If you knew Tommy three hundred years ago, why isn't he grown up? He still looks like a teenager."

"It's the way things are here in the pirate realm," her aunt answered. "The pirates get a choice of when they want to grow up."

"Aye," Eddie said, "and growin' up is something a man needs to take some time at. Be choosy about when he's goin' to do it."

"Get him down from there," Zelda instructed Eddie. "We've got to gather the rest of the crew."

"Aye." Eddie started for the side of the street where the tightrope walker was headed.

The wind stirred Tommy Hawkeyes's shoulder-length black hair. He was ten feet from the other end of the rope when a window on the balcony it was tied to opened.

Another young man shoved his head and shoulders through the window. An angry expression twisted his face. "Well now, you unlovely jack-anapes," the new arrival said. "Looks like I've caught you between a rock and a hard place."

Tommy Hawkeyes grinned. "An' if ye're so sure of that, Will Donner, whyn't ye come on out here and give me the comeuppance ye think I so richly deserve yerself?"

"Tommy!"

Sabrina recognized the note of concern and authority in Aunt Zelda's voice.

Tommy's head came around in surprise, and for a moment Sabrina thought he was going to plummet from the tightrope. "Zellie!" he called down in excited surprise. "I heard ye was a-comin', but I wasn't sure if'n it was true."

"It's true. Now get down here before you get hurt." Zelda put her hands on her hips.

Tommy recovered his balance and stood on the tightrope. His eyes squinted. "Ye've *changed*, Zellie." He didn't sound happy about it. "Why would ye go and do somethin' like that?"

"We can discuss that later."

"I got time to discuss it now."

"No you don't," Will Donner said. The other boy climbed from the balcony window and slowly walked out onto the tightrope. He carried a long knife in one hand.

"Tommy," Zelda called.

"In a minute," Tommy replied. "I got to put this struttin' popinjay in his place again. Got a great stone block for a head and doesn't much like to listen to reason."

He's not the only one, Sabrina thought as she watched. Even though she feared for Tommy, so high above the street, there was something exciting about watching him. He was so confident, so daring. It was like nothing she'd seen before.

"Come on out here with ye, then," Tommy dared. "I ain't goin' to wait on ye all day."

"Well, he's certainly sure of himself," Hilda said beside Sabrina.

"The audience isn't." Salem pointed a paw at the area under the tightrope as the people that had gathered there suddenly pushed back.

"Tommy never has known fear," Zelda said. A smile turned her lips. "He's always been like that."

Looking at her aunt, Sabrina suddenly realized that Tommy and Zelda had probably been about the same age back during Zelda's pirating days. *A shipboard romance?* The possibility sounded kind of yummy and definitely made Sabrina want to ask more, but she also knew Zelda didn't tell anything more than she wanted to.

Will Donner held on to the balcony with one hand, swaying a little uncertainly on the tightrope. He waved his knife menacingly, but he was still three feet short of Tommy.

"C'mon out," Tommy taunted.

"Common cur," Will Donner shouted. "If you weren't such a coward, you'd fight me."

"Oh," Tommy said, standing easily on the thick

hawser rope. He twirled the parasol nonchalantly. "Ye with yer pigsticker and me with me bare hands?" He shook his head. "Maybe it's just me, Will, but it doesn't sound like a fair fight." He smiled. "I'll not be a-takin' advantage of you that way."

Below the tightrope, the crowd laughed appreciatively. Several of them hollered at Will Donner, making fun of his reluctance to step out onto the tightrope.

"He's really something, isn't he?" Hilda asked.

"Stupid comes to mind," Salem said. "He is, after all, standing on a rope. If the other guy ever stops to realize that, it wouldn't take long for that knife to cut through that rope."

Sabrina wrapped her hand around Salem's muzzle. "Shhh," the teen witch said. "I don't think he needs your help."

"Well, Will," Tommy said, shrugging, "if ye aren't a-gonna come to me, why then I'll just mosey on over that way." He closed the parasol and crossed the rope.

Chapter 7

Heart in her throat, Sabrina watched as the young pirate walked the tightrope toward his would-be attacker.

As soon as Tommy was within reach, Will Donner struck with his knife. Surefooted and brimming with lighthearted confidence, Tommy blocked the knife thrust with the gay parasol.

"Oho," Tommy chortled, "an' ye are serious about this little fracas, aren't ye?"

"She was my girl," Will Donner shouted, sweeping the knife toward Tommy's face again. "You would have done well to steer clear of her."

Tommy parried the blow with ease. "An' that's not what she told me, you big lunk. Seemed to me she was a free spirit. An' a mighty lovely one at that."

The crowd shouted out with approval again as Will Donner's face turned beet red. Sabrina marveled at the reaction. The audience treated the life-

or-death encounter like it was nothing but entertainment. But it sounded a lot like the WWF, too.

Tommy stayed close to the other boy. The parasol danced in the young pirate's hand like a live thing, parrying and blocking the other boy's blows easily. The parasol's umbrella turned to tatters, though.

Ahead, Eddie suddenly abandoned his pursuit of Tommy and returned to Zelda's side with a concerned expression. "I'm afraid we've been undone, Zellie." He pointed with his chin toward a half-dozen governor's guardsmen approaching them from ahead. "An' it looks just as bad back the way we come."

Sabrina glanced over her shoulder and saw another dozen of the Governor's Patrol coming up behind them. The large lady, Jasmine, was with them. Jasmine gestured at Black Eddie Peas, talking excitedly.

"It looks like she knows you," Sabrina said.

"Aye," Eddie said. "Though I really thought she wouldn't remember." He glanced around and nodded toward an alley between a glassblower's shop and a paint supply store. "Perhaps we have a way out if we're about it quick enough."

Sabrina looked at the hard-faced guards. *Now is not a good time to be without magic.* She adjusted her backpack straps, feeling Salem shifting inside.

Above, Tommy Hawkeyes continued dueling with Will Donner. The crowd clapped in admiration, perhaps even thinking they were just getting another show. The Governor's Patrol wasn't interested in the high-wire tableau; they closed in quietly and quickly, shoving their way through the crowd. The people in the street thought about pushing back, but when they saw it was the patrol, they quickly stepped aside.

Eddie cupped his hands around his mouth and lifted his voice. "Tommy! Tommy, lad!"

Tommy blocked with the parasol and stepped back on the tightrope quickly. He glanced down and saw Eddie, who pointed out the patrol members. "Go on. I'll catch up with you."

Turning quickly, Eddie gestured to the three witches and headed toward the alley. Seeing that their quarry was attempting to escape, the Governor's Patrol bared their swords and shoved their way through the crowd. The patrol members knocked people down and raced over them.

"Go!" Eddie said, waving the witches down the alley. He halted by a filled apple cart. Bracing himself, grunting with effort, the big pirate caught hold of the cart and turned it over on its side.

Apples spilled from the cart, rolling across the hard-packed dirt of the street. Patrol members, as well as people rushing to get out of their way, tripped over the rolling apples and crashed to the ground.

Sabrina paused at the alley entrance and glanced up.

Tommy blocked Will Donner's latest attempt

with the knife, then reversed the parasol so the curved handle was thrust out. He blocked the next attack, then hooked Will Donner's hand with the curved end and yanked. The knife spun free in the air, and Tommy caught it effortlessly with his free hand.

"C'mon, girlie," Eddie growled, taking Sabrina's arm.

"Let's go," Salem urged.

Sabrina resisted long enough to watch Tommy slash the tightrope beneath his feet, grabbing one end of it. Will Donner scrambled, hurried, barely catching hold of the balcony as the tightrope dropped.

Tommy swung from the long section of the rope to the other side of the street, arching out to land on a green-and-white striped awning above the glassblower's shop. The knife flicked out and sliced through the awning's support ropes. Freed, the awning fluttered down and draped the patrol members on the other side of the overturned apple cart. The young pirate let go of the awning support hooks and flipped, landing only a couple of feet from Sabrina.

"So what do ye think about that?" Tommy asked the teen witch, a broad grin on his face.

Sabrina glanced at the patrol members struggling under the heavy tarp. "Pretty cool." A sword blade suddenly shoved through the material and cut a slit. "Only it's not going to hold them long." She turned and ran down the alley, following Eddie's pull.

The alley was long and narrow and crooked. Multicolored cats dashed out of the way, squalling in alarm and anger. Rats scurried in piles of refuse stacked behind different buildings. Narrow wooden fire escapes tracked up the sides of the structures on either side of the alley.

Zelda led the way, and from the decisive way she moved, Sabrina could tell that her aunt knew the layout of the town. Even with the overturned apple cart and the dropped awning, the patrol members poured into the alley after them.

The alley turned quickly to the right. After entering the turn, Sabrina's view was blocked for a moment. The other end of the alley loomed ahead, opening onto another market area.

"Over this way," an old man's voice advised. A leathery hand stretched from the back door of a business. "Got a safe place where you can hide out."

Zelda hesitated for just a moment, then looked more closely at the man. "Abner?"

The old man grinned, baring snaggled teeth. "Aye. Surprised you still remember me, it's been so long."

Zelda led the way through the door, followed by Hilda and Sabrina. Tommy and Eddie brought up the rear. Abner closed the door behind them.

Sabrina glanced around the small room, barely making out the details in the darkness. Shelves covered the walls, filled with jars of canned food and baking supplies. The scent of spices overlaid everything, tickling Sabrina's nose. Everyone was breathing so hard that Sabrina was certain the Governor's Patrol would hear as they rushed by.

Then the drone of running feet echoed in the alley outside. Sabrina's heart beat frantically when she heard the patrol members slow.

"Where'd they go?" someone asked outside.

Eddie tightened his grip on his cutlass, and Tommy fisted the knife he'd stolen. Abner quietly put a large board in the L-shaped brackets on the door to bar the entrance. The old man walked to the wall to the right and pressed a hidden button.

The wall clicked loudly in the small dark room, then came forward a little and turned to reveal a small, secret hallway beyond. Abner waved them toward the hallway.

Aunt Zelda knows this guy, Sabrina thought. *Everything's going to be okay.* Still, she was beginning to really wish she'd stayed home in Westbridge. But if she'd known what kind of trouble her aunts were going to get into, she knew she wouldn't have been happy there either.

The teen witch followed Hilda and Zelda into the gloomy hallway. Abner closed the secret door behind them, and the hallway was totally dark. Sabrina tripped over the uneven floor and almost fell. She didn't feel safe at all.

"Search the alley," someone ordered outside. "You men go ahead into the market and see if you can find them there. Be quick about it. Governor Leroy will have our heads if we don't find them."

Sabrina swallowed hard and glanced at Eddie. "That's a joke, right?"

"Ah, girlie," the rugged pirate said, "in truth, I don't know. The governor works for Queen Becca, and she's an ill-tempered woman. Her and Feargus the Second used to have somethin' of a dalliance a-goin', but one or the other broke it off. No one knows which. Now they spend their time a-tryin' to get back at each other."

Abner scuttled forward in the hallway and paused to take down a small oil lamp from the wall. He struck a match and lit the wick, closing the hurricane glass back down.

Weak golden light burned through the darkness. The hallway was narrow and crooked, the flooring slapped together from wooden remnants that overlapped. At the end of the hallway, a ladder thrust up from a hole in the floor.

"Down here," Abner said, taking hold of the ladder and starting down, "and be quick about it. The patrol will probably be through that door in a few minutes. If we get lucky, maybe they won't find the trick door. But I'd rather put some distance between us and them."

Hilda followed next, then Zelda. Sabrina stepped onto the ladder and felt it shaking as her aunts climbed down. She hoped it would hold. Abner's lamp seemed a surprisingly long way down.

"Easy, easy," Salem cautioned.

"Maybe you'd like to climb this on your own," Sabrina suggested. Tommy swung onto the ladder above her, sending a new tremor through it. She held her breath for a moment, then continued climbing down.

Could sea monsters, even Old Agnes, be any worse than this?

"This is an old smuggler's route," Abner said as he held the oil lamp up to light the way. The weak yellow light poured down the stone passageway. A small stream, glistening silver in the lamplight, trickled through the center of the passageway.

Sabrina guessed that the passageway was at least eight feet in diameter, because the walls were a couple of feet outside her arms' reach. She walked along the sloped side just outside the running water. A cool wind blew through the passageway, bringing the brine smell of the ocean.

"This passageway goes out to the ocean?" Sabrina asked.

"Aye," Abner replied, peering ahead. He peered at faded chalk marks on the wall, tracing them with his finger as if to make certain of them. "If you follow it long enough. Fresh air comes from a few blow holes that have been made along the way, but the main entrance for smugglers' goods is underwater about a mile from here."

"Underwater?" Images of the elasmosaurus filled Sabrina's mind. She didn't want to go into the water.

Abner laughed dryly. "Don't you worry your pretty head. We aren't going that far."

Sabrina glanced at the chalk marks on the stone wall, noticing another passageway branching off the one they walked down.

Abner paused only a little farther ahead. He raised the oil lamp to peer more closely at four passageways ahead, then chose the second from the left.

"There are a lot of passageways down here," Sabrina said nervously.

"Aye," the old man replied. "Whole island's honeycombed with them. Some of them were natural, caused by the island's formation thousands of years ago, but pirates have added to them since. The governor and Queen Becca closed a lot of them by sending demolition teams down here."

"They blew up tunnels?" Sabrina asked, stepping into the new passageway.

"Of course. They find it hard to put a tax on supplies and goods they never see shipped onto or off the island. And there's a certain amount of contraband that comes onto the island. Books and papers about the bad things the queen and governor are doing. Secrets they'd rather not have everyone know. As well as spies for King Feargus the Second."

"So how safe is this?" Sabrina asked.

"Pretty safe." Abner sounded nonchalant. "As long as you know where you're going." He stopped suddenly. "Ooops."

"Ooops?" Sabrina said. "*Ooops* isn't good. Ooops isn't something I want to hear while we're walking around in almost total darkness with the possibility of cave-ins." Then she saw the sudden drop-off the old man stood in front of. Hypnotized by it, the teen witch went forward and peered down.

The drop-off looked endless. She accidentally kicked a rock over the edge. It bounced a couple of times, echoing in the passageway, and made a liquid *bloop* far below.

Abner shined his lamp down into the drop-off. The bottom remained beyond the reach of the light. "*Ooops* beats the splat of the sudden stop at the end of a long fall. Looks like I made a wrong turn. We'll have to go back."

"Nobody," Sabrina said, "mentioned any bottomless pits when we came down here."

"Maybe," Tommy suggested, "you'd have preferred staying and talking to the Governor's Patrol."

"No." Sabrina followed Abner back from the drop-off. "I'm just saying I wasn't fully informed."

"Oh," Abner said. "I can tell you about the spiders and blood leeches that live down here if you want. And then there's some of the queen's laboratory rats and experiments that are said to have been shoved down here to get rid of them."

Sabrina shivered. "Okay, maybe you can be too informed."

"I haven't been down here much." Abner shined the oil lamp at another juncture of passageways. He chose the one on the right and went forward.

Sabrina hesitated for only a moment, looking at

the chalk marks she didn't understand. Then she went on. She hated not having any real choices herself.

"Some of us managed to escape Feargus the Second's trap," Abner went on as they followed the downward slope of the new tunnel. "Me, Tommy, a handful of others. First thing we did was get the ship's crew that stayed in Bertie's Waddle after Ol' Agnes took the Cap'n."

"Aye," Eddie grumbled. "Those were the crew that didn't want no part of our shippin' venture."

"We all figured you were going to get caught," Abner admitted. "Cap'n Cutter was an intelligent man. You remember how he was, don't you, Zellie? Always and forever planning. If it hadn't been for Ol' Agnes, King Feargus and Queen Becca would never have laid a hand on our ship."

"Yes," Zelda answered.

Abner stopped and looked back at her. "You don't think badly of us for giving up on the ship with the Cap'n gone, do you?" The old man's lined face showed worry.

Sabrina felt sorry for him.

"No," Zelda answered. "You did what you thought you needed to."

Tears glistened in the old man's eyes. "I did. I really did."

"Aye, you old dog," Eddie said in a gentler voice. He patted the old man's shoulder. "An' if'n ye had a-sailed with us, look at the pickle ye woulda been in now."

Abner nodded and wiped his face. "I come to Governor's Island when I heard you had the ship and were going looking for the Ootnannian treasure."

Eddie scowled as they continued down the passageway. "We still got a problem. King Feargus kept our mates, an' he stuck me with a bunch of his navy boys."

"I know," Abner said. "We've seen them."

" 'We've' seen them?" Zelda asked.

"Sure," Abner said. "After I heard that the ship had been taken and that Eddie was being made to search for the treasure, I gathered up the ship's crew that had split off after the Cap'n was taken. They're all here on the island. Calico Tom. Long Bones McGee. Herman. Zigzag Crowder. They're all here, Eddie. We were just waiting for you to get back from wherever you'd been."

"We didn't know ye had gone for Zellie, though," Tommy said. He walked at Hilda's side, occasionally helping her over the rougher areas. "Next to Cap'n Cutter, she was the best at plannin' attacks and raids."

Sabrina glanced back at Hilda, who looked totally surprised.

"Who knew?" Hilda whispered.

"Ye got the rest of the crew?" Eddie asked. "When I saw Tommy a-walkin' that tightropes, I had hopes."

"Aye," Abner said. "That's where I'm taking you now. Tommy was our lookout. He entertained folks down near the harbor so he'd know most of the comings and goings of ships, goods, and folks. All of us were standing by."

"Where is the crew?" Zelda asked.

Abner held the oil lamp up. The light revealed a set of stone steps cut into the wall at the end of the passageway. They led up to a wooden trapdoor. "Here. If nothing has gone wrong." He started up the stone steps.

Suddenly, a loud detonation ripped through the passageway, shaking Abner from the stone steps. The thunderous blast deafened Sabrina for a moment, and she thought the stone floor beneath her was going to collapse. She fell heavily against the stone wall, drawing a flurry of complaints from Salem.

"The Governor's Patrol," Tommy said after the detonation died away. "They must know we've made it down into the smugglers' caves."

"All the more reason not to be here when they come this way," Abner said grimly. He started up the stone steps again. When he opened the trapdoor above, stern-faced men bristling with knives, swords, and flintlock pistols met him.

For a heartbeat—or a couple of dozen—Sabrina wasn't sure; she just knew they were all in trouble. Then she realized the men weren't wearing the Governor's Patrol uniforms.

The scarred and stern faces of the men above suddenly broke into broad smiles. "Abner!" a large black pirate yelled out in glee. "When we heard the patrol was after ye, we'd about thought ye were done for!" He reached down into the trapdoor and hauled the old man out.

"No," Abner crowed. "I brought a few friends, though." He gestured proudly down into the trapdoor.

"Zellie!" another pirate called out happily. "Glad to have ye among us again!" Someone extended a hand down and helped Zelda up.

Sabrina went up after Hilda, followed by Eddie and Tommy. The large room around them turned out to be a warehouse. Stacks of wooden crates reached nearly to the ceiling twenty feet above.

The pirates hugged Zelda with glee, all of them talking in excited voices. Most of the brief bits of conversation that Sabrina overheard concerned tales of adventure that she would have loved to hear— but not while they were being chased by the Governor's Patrol.

"Well," Hilda said, sounding somewhat jealous, "I guess she's going to be the life of the party around here."

"Don't ye be a-worryin' yer noggin about that," Eddie exclaimed. "Ye will find yer a-gonna fit right in with the ship's crew. I've already developed a fondness for ye meself." The big pirate hugged Hilda with one arm, then went to join the others.

"You know," Hilda said, smiling, "I really think I'm going to put this place on my vacation list."

Another sudden explosion bellowed deep in the passageways. This blast was much closer. Roiling dust clouds spurted from the open trapdoor, and flying pebbles rattled against nearby crates.

Sabrina ducked and covered her head. She looked at Hilda. "Maybe you should hold off on your vacation plans until things have quieted down around here."

"Okay," Zelda said, getting to her feet, "staying here is probably out of the question. Where is our ship now?"

Chapter 8

☆

"I say we should rush them, knives in our teeth, pistols at the ready. Give no quarter and ask none in return." They were seated on a crate near the dock where the pirate ship sat at anchor. King Feargus the Second's naval forces presently held *Screamin' Mimi,* Captain Cutter's ship. Sentries walked the ship's deck carrying flintlock rifles. Salem gazed around at all the pirates watching him. "What do you say, me hearties? Are you with me?"

The pirates gazed at the cat in total disbelief.

"No," Long Bones McGee answered. "What kind of daft plan is that?"

"It's actually a good plan," Salem argued. "I took a lot of prize ships in my day just like this."

Sabrina gazed out into the harbor. Night had fallen over an hour ago. They had managed to evade the Governor's Patrol by staying in the different hiding places the pirates had discovered on the island. However, if they were going to get off the island, they had to have the ship.

"Ye know," Tommy said, "at first I thought the idea of a talkin' cat was the stupidest thing I'd ever heard. Then the cat had to go and open its mouth." He shook his head.

"And you have the gall to call yourself pirates," Salem accused sarcastically. "In my day, pirates were a vicious and bloodthirsty lot. They were men other men feared, the kind of men who gave children and small animals nightmares."

"Salem," Zelda admonished, "that will be enough. We have plenty of problems without you making them worse."

"So now we're going to blame the cat," Salem griped.

Tommy leaned in close to the cat. He ran a calloused thumb over his knife's edge. "I been a-thinkin' that maybe I need some new socks. I'm kind of partial to furry ones."

Sabrina quickly picked Salem up and returned him to her backpack. She liked Tommy, but she wasn't sure if the pirate boy was joking.

"Well, if'n we're not a-gonna rush the ship, what are we a-gonna do?" Eddie watched *Screamin' Mimi* in disgust.

Men's voices lifted in song carried all over the harbor. Only a few of the ships still had men busy loading or unloading cargo. Most of the other ships' crews appeared to be partying. The taverns along the docks looked filled to capacity.

"Too bad they didn't all just go to a party," Sabrina said.

"They can't," Eddie said. "A captain always leaves a skeleton crew aboard to protect the ship."

"True, but the party could go to the skeleton crew." Zelda looked at *Screamin' Mimi* with renewed interest. "And, even though we can't use our powers thanks to the Shield of the Amazing Bob, we can still make a sleeping potion that should do quite nicely. Abner, I'm going to need a few ingredients."

"Aye, Zellie," the old man said, grinning. "Did I ever let you down as ship's quartermaster before?"

Zelda quickly gave him her list.

"A sleeping potion," Salem grumbled irritably. He sniffed disdainfully. "Some pirates."

"Just let me do the talking," Zelda whispered as she led the way to the pirate ship.

Sabrina felt a little nervous, not being used to the life of a fugitive. While Abner had been out gathering the supplies her aunt had requested, and while Zelda and Hilda had been busy making a sleeping potion, the Governor's Patrol had come through the docks twice. If Eddie and his group were still on the island by morning, Sabrina felt certain they would be captured.

Arm in arm with Abner, Zelda started up the boardwalk leading to *Screamin' Mimi*. They didn't get far before they were challenged by one of the sentries.

"Halt! Who goes there?" The sentry blocked their

way at the top of the boardwalk. Two other sentries joined the first, bringing their weapons to bear.

Zelda looked at the men in feigned surprise. "Oh, I'm so sorry. We must have the wrong ship. You know, they all look alike in the dark."

"Aye, ma'am," the sentry responded. "I suppose a ship can look much like another to an untrained eye."

"Excuse us. We'll be going down. Sorry to be any trouble." Zelda turned and started to go back down the boardwalk.

"Zellie," Abner protested, "we've direly inconvenienced these young men. Surely we could offer them some recompense for our mistake." The old man held up the ale jug he carried. "How about it, lads? Would you like to wet your whistle to whatever moves you this night? Trust me when I say I've had to stand guard a few nights myself while the rest of the crew got leave."

The sentry hesitated for only a moment, then took the jug.

Zelda and Abner led the small party of witches and pirates down the dock till they were out of sight.

"Now," Zelda said, "we shouldn't have long to wait."

Less than an hour later, Sabrina helped Abner roll the last of the sleeping Ootnannian sailors into the cargo net spread out in the center of *Screamin' Mimi*'s deck. The pirates had already carried eleven other men there.

"Haul away," Black Eddie Peas called out.

Instantly, the lines holding the cargo net drew taut. The net wrapped around the sleeping sailors and lifted them from the ship's deck. Quickly, the pirates put the net over the side and gently let it down on the docks in the middle of a stack of crates.

Sabrina watched in fascination as Zelda strode to the stern castle deck and started giving orders. The pirates swarmed up the rigging and ratlines. The masts and yardarms filled with sailcloth in minutes. Thankfully, the winds came across the island, making it easy for them to get out of the harbor. They lit lanterns so they could be seen and to warn other ships.

Salem bounded from Sabrina's backpack and ran to the railing, peering over the side. The cat's hair ruffled in the breeze.

Screamin' Mimi moved sedately through the water, heading out to sea. She passed by ships on both sides, drawing friendly wishes from other crews. The pirate ship had a totally different feel to Sabrina than the cargo ship had. *Screamin' Mimi* felt smooth and sleek, not bouncing, cutting through the water.

Excitement filled Sabrina as she realized they were free—at least for the moment. The twin guard towers and the chain-link fence still closed the harbor off.

The teen witch dashed through the flurry of men and up the steps to join Zelda.

Her aunt stood at the railing. Her voice was calm as she spoke, but it bristled with authority. "Abner, I'll need a list of ship's stores, what we have and what we don't. Once we get out past the Shield's radius getting things won't be a problem with my powers, but I want to be certain we can make it."

"Aye, Cap'n," the quartermaster replied, hustling off.

"Eddie, I want a crew list. Don't worry about information on people I know, just give me their names. As for the ones I don't know, I want a list of what kind of experience they have."

"Aye, Cap'n." Eddie hurried down the steps, yelling at men still hanging in the rigging.

"And, Eddie," Zelda called down, "I'll want a cleaning detail put together right after that."

The burly pirate wasn't as quick about responding then, and his, "Aye, Cap'n," lacked enthusiasm.

Sabrina stepped up beside her aunt. "Should I call you Captain, too?"

Zelda's face softened, losing some of the worry that had seemed to take root there once she'd linked back up with the pirate crew. "Only if you want to."

"I was just wondering."

"It's just a lot of responsibility, Sabrina," Zelda said, looking out at the two guard towers. "It's funny looking back on it. That summer I was convinced that I was running away from responsibility when I jumped ship and joined the pirates. I just didn't know I'd end up being second-in-command of a pirate ship. And now, I'm not sure that I want to do this at all."

"Once we get out past the effects of the shield," Sabrina said, "we could go back."

Zelda was quiet for a moment. "I can't. Without

Captain Cutter, these men would be lost. King Feargus has part of the crew, and he isn't joking about punishing them if Eddie doesn't find the treasure." She looked at Sabrina. "You and Hilda could go back, if you want. In fact, I think I'd prefer it. Neither of you are prepared for this."

Sabrina shook her head. "I couldn't leave you here."

"Neither could I," Hilda said. "I don't think you could get rid of either of us at this point."

"Thank you," Zelda said in a husky voice. "Thank you both." She reached out for them. All three witches group-hugged.

"Oh fine," Salem said, sitting on the railing. He'd obviously made his way around the ship. "A family moment and we're excluding the cat."

"*He*," all three witches said at the same time, "could go." Then they tried to hide their laughter.

"Very funny," Salem said, blinking his yellow eyes. "But you guys are going to one day realize what an asset I am to this little adventure of yours. I just hope for your sakes that it's not too late."

"Personally," Hilda said, "I can't imagine us ever being that desperate."

"Speaking of desperate situations," Sabrina said, "what are we going to do about the guard towers?"

"They'll let us out," Zelda said. "Getting in is the hard part."

Still, as calm as Zelda was about the situation, Sabrina didn't relax till the chain-link gate parted and *Screamin' Mimi* sailed through without interruption.

"Okay," Sabrina said, letting out a tense breath, "what now?" She looked back the way they had come, watching the lighted guard towers growing dimmer behind them.

"Now," Zelda said, "we get *Screamin' Mimi* shipshape again and go looking for Old Agnes."

Neither of those options, Sabrina decided, *sounds like anything I want to do. Cleaning or sea monsters? Some choice.*

The sounds of men's voices raised in near-mutiny levels woke Sabrina the next morning. With that much hysteria in their voices, she felt certain *Screamin' Mimi* was under attack.

She struggled up from the gently swinging hammock in the captain's cabin she'd shared with her aunts. Cautiously, she made her way over to the porthole and peered out. A seemingly endless expanse of blue green spread out before her. Whitecapped waves rolled toward the ship's side, falling behind in the twisting wake of the ship. Gulls cried as they winged up from behind the ship and passed through her view.

Okay, no sea monsters in sight. Sabrina let out a relaxed breath. *That only leaves what? Other pirates? The governor's men? King Feargus the Second's navy?*

The deck rolled underfoot as *Screamin' Mimi* gently rose and fell. Sabrina walked over to the door and opened it slightly.

The pirates stood amidships in orderly rows, their

eyes wide with terror. Zelda stood before them. Steam rose from mop buckets.

"This ship is a pigsty," her aunt was saying. The morning light revealed that the statement was true. The ship was crudded over with dirt and grime. Loose coils of rope lay across the deck. Gulls picked over bits of food lodged in cracks.

"It weren't us, Cap'n," one grizzled old mate protested. "It was them Ootnannian sailors what made this mess. Ye know Cap'n Cutter, may he live long to give Ol' Agnes terrible indigestion, would never let *Mimi* look like this."

Zelda stepped up to the man, pushing her face only inches from his. Her hands rested on her hips. "I know that, sailor—and I'm using that term loosely. We're on a mission to find Cap'n Cutter, and I won't have him seeing his ship in such a state. It would probably be enough to make him crawl right back down Old Agnes's gullet. Do I make myself clear?"

The pirate nodded, his ruddy complexion paling. His eyes didn't meet Zelda's. "Aye, Cap'n. Hearin' you good an' loud."

Wow, Sabrina thought. *Now this is a side of Aunt Zelda I've never seen.* It suddenly made her realize her life as a teenager could have been drastically different.

"Perfect," Zelda said. "Now I want every one of you men to grab a mop and pail and get busy. I want *Mimi* cleaned from stem to stern."

Black Eddie Peas raised his voice. "An' if'n any

of you give the cap'n a bit of sass, I'm a-gonna see to it personally that—"

"Mr. Peas," Zelda's voice cracked.

Eddie froze, blinking his eyes owlishly. "Aye, Cap'n."

"Stow that bilge," Zelda ordered. "There's only one captain on this deck, and I can back up anything I say."

Eddie nodded. "Aye, Cap'n. Sorry, Cap'n."

"Stop apologizing and grab a bucket," Zelda said. "You're wasting valuable cleaning time."

Eddie took up a bucket and fell in with the other pirates. They all grumbled for a short time, but did so in low breaths that didn't carry far. After a time, though, someone started singing.

Ninety-nine bottles of ale on the wall,
Ninety-nine bottles of ale.
Take one down and pass it around.
Ninety-eight bottles of ale on the wall.

It wasn't long before the other pirates joined in.

Despite the noise, Sabrina thought she might be able to crawl back into the hammock for a little more sleep. After yesterday, she was really tired. She started to close the door quietly so her aunt wouldn't hear.

"Sabrina," Zelda called without turning around. "I know you're awake."

Busted. Sabrina sighed, knowing sleep was now out of the question.

"I need every able-bodied person on board if we're going to do this," Zelda said. "Get down to the galley and get some breakfast, then I'll need you here."

"Aye, Cap'n." Sabrina closed the door and returned to the cabin. She peered into the mirror above the small desk built into the wall. Her hair was tossed and tangled. She blew a lock out of her face in disgust. *This sure isn't an ocean cruise.*

She pointed at her hair, hoping they were out of range of the Shield of the Amazing Bob. *Sproing!* Her finger felt slightly numb, letting her know she still couldn't do magic. She whined in disgust, then reached into her backpack for the brush and change of clothes she had there.

Trapped aboard a dirty pirate ship that was wanted by two kingdoms and captained by Aunt Bligh on a sea filled with monsters wasn't a good thing. It couldn't get any worse. Could it?

Chapter 9

*O*kay, Sabrina sighed, *maybe things aren't getting any worse, but they're definitely not getting any better either.* The runny eggs sloshed slowly on her tin plate, imitating the rise and fall of the Gentle Sea. Sighing, she mopped them up with a piece of dry toast and ate. The bacon seemed to be all gristle and chewed like leather.

Aunt Hilda came through the galley doors wearing a grease-stained apron. Her hair was matted under a cook's hat. "How's your breakfast?"

Sabrina choked the bite of toast down. "Ummm, did you make this?"

"No. Abner did." Hilda gathered up a stack of dirty dishes left on one of the nearby tables. She blew a wisp of hair from her face. "I drew dishes. Do you know how many dishes hungry pirates can dirty?"

Sabrina shook her head, not really wanting to

know. She cut up her pancakes, poured more maple syrup over them, and finished them off as well. More than anything, she wanted more sleep. As weird as the hammock had been to sleep in, it had been comfortable. She smothered a yawn.

The galley was a large, rectangular room. Tables with benches on brackets were fastened to the floor. Food stained the walls and floor.

"Aren't we going to be out from under the Shield of the Amazing Bob soon?" Sabrina piled her plate on the stack on her table, then helped Hilda carry them back to the dishwashing area.

"I was in favor of waiting till we got our powers back," her aunt admitted. "But I was overruled by our captain. In case we do run into trouble, she wants *Screamin' Mimi* clean."

The dishwashing area lined one wall opposite the stoves and flat grill. Abner and two other men stirred big pots and cut up vegetables.

Sabrina set her stack of plates down on the water-dappled surface by the two water reservoirs. "What kind of trouble can we run into out here? I mean, aside from sea monsters, including Old Agnes."

"According to Zelda, we won't find Old Agnes out here." Hilda scooted some of the dishes into the first reservoir's soapy water. "We're going to find her in the Sargasso of Lost Ships."

"This is a place?"

"It's where Old Agnes has been stashing the ships she's taken for the last forty years. Zelda was told that Old Agnes makes a nest every five or six hundred years to lay her eggs."

"There's going to be more Old Agneses?" The thought sent shivers down Sabrina's back.

"Most of the eggs never hatch," Hilda replied, scrubbing the first of the dishes. Steam wafted up from the hot, soapy water.

"Maybe it's just me," Sabrina said, helping scrub, "but I'm thinking being around a mommy sea monster with a brand-new baby is probably not a good thing."

"Zelda figures it will be another fifty years or so before the babies hatch. And besides, that's where Captain Cutter is."

"How far are we from the Sargasso of Lost Ships?"

"Another two or three days of sailing."

"Two or three days?" Sabrina couldn't believe it. *I can't do dishes and scrub for that long!*

"Yes," Hilda replied.

Sabrina washed a plate angrily, getting it extra clean. "Will we still have time to get back to Westbridge before Sunday?" Time flowed differently in parts of the Other Realm, allowing witches and warlocks to carry on lives there, as well as in the mortal realm. "I've got a date with Harvey."

"We'll have plenty of time," Hilda said. "I think."

"You think?"

Her aunt nodded. "I'm pretty sure."

That wasn't what Sabrina wanted to hear. As they

worked on the dishes, the teen witch kept getting images of Harvey knocking on the door of the empty Spellman house. *He'll probably think I'm mad at him. Poor Harvey.*

"You'd think that since it's in the water all this time, the ship couldn't get dirty." Sabrina was on her hands and knees, scrubbing at the accumulated grime on the railing with a toothbrush. At least the toothbrush wasn't hers.

"The sea is hard on ships," Zelda said distractedly. She stood at the navigation table next to the big wheel that controlled *Screamin' Mimi*'s huge rudder. Her attention was locked on the curling maps she'd spread out with both hands. A protractor rested lightly on the parchment. "Corrosion can eat the metal parts away. The sun can rot the rigging and sailcloth, drying it out time after time when it gets wet. And barnacles can weaken a ship's hull if they're allowed to build up for too long. That's some of the first things you learn about being a sailor."

The sound of men singing came up and over the stern railing.

Seventy-six bottles of ale on the wall,
Seventy-six bottles of ale.
Take one down and pass it around.
Seventy-five bottles of ale on the wall.

Zelda glared over the stern railing. "The second thing you learn is probably that annoying song."

Sabrina silently agreed. They were well into their second day of the journey, still not quite out of reach of the Shield of the Amazing Bob. During waking hours, when Zelda assigned the crew duties, they sang constantly. *Screamin' Mimi* wasn't even quiet at night, when Sabrina was so tired from cleaning that she'd drop into her hammock and fall instantly asleep.

The pirate ship was looking a lot cleaner, Sabrina had to admit, but she was beginning to feel like Cinderella.

"Have you figured out how we're going to get Captain Cutter back from Old Agnes?" Sabrina asked.

Zelda sighed, sounding totally worn out. "No. I've never talked to her, so all I have to go on are the stories I've heard about her. They're not flattering, of course, but surely there's some part of her that can be reasoned with." She paused. "I hope."

Looking at her aunt, Sabrina suddenly realized that she always went to sleep before Zelda and always woke up after her. Zelda had pulled marathons before while doing research or experiments with her science projects, but Sabrina didn't think she'd ever seen her aunt so close to exhaustion.

Suddenly, a tingle raced through Sabrina. She glanced up at her aunt. "Did you feel that?"

A small smile lit Zelda's face. "Indeed I did."

"Does that mean what I think it does?" Sabrina stretched out her grime-encrusted hand excitedly.

"Yes, it does. I believe your days with the tooth-brush are finally over." Zelda rolled the maps she'd been studying and walked to the stern castle railing.

Sabrina followed, enjoying the warm buzz that filled her. She glanced down and saw the pirates busily scrubbing and mopping the deck amidships.

"Eddie," Zelda called.

"Aye, Cap'n." Eddie squinted up at her, looking really tired himself.

"Have your cleaning crews stand down." Zelda waited while the order was given.

The pirates gladly gave up their mops, buckets, and scrub brushes, sagging tiredly against the railing. Despite the obnoxious song and their ability to sing it for what seemed forever, Sabrina knew they were tired, too.

Zelda pointed with authority and said,

Winds may change and winds may blow,
But we'll be clean wherever we go.
Scrub brushes skate and mops dance,
Screamin' Mimi *you should enhance.*

Immediately, the mops stood up in ranks. Sabrina got the impression they would have saluted if they'd had arms. The mops jumped into buckets, soaked themselves thoroughly, and flashed across the decks, leaving trails of soapy suds. The scrub brushes followed like excited puppies, racing along after the mops.

The pirates seemed stunned for just a moment, then they began singing again in boisterous, if not exactly tuneful, voices. Some of them even paired off and started dancing arm in arm.

A rover 'pon the sea,
Now that's the life for the likes o' me!
Gimme silver,
Gimme gold,
Gimme fortunes with wealth untold!
Aye, matie, a pirate's what I wanna be!

A dog howled mournfully in the distance, drawing Sabrina's attention immediately. "I didn't know we had a dog on board," she said.

"We don't," Zelda replied, "but when singing is that badly off-key, a dog will hear it somewhere in the Other Realm and lodge a protest."

"Oh." Still, it was easy to want to join in with the pirates' revelry. "Well, maybe they just need a little direction." Sabrina pointed up a new pirate ensemble for herself, black pants tucked into knee-high roll-top boots and a sea green shirt with belled sleeves. She also washed, dried, and styled her hair into a French braid with another point. She started to head down the stairs.

"Wait just a minute, Sabrina."

Sabrina's enthusiasm dropped. That tone of voice never meant anything good.

"Eddie and the others may be done for a while," Zelda said firmly, "but our jobs have just begun if

we want to get *Screamin' Mimi* properly outfitted."
She paused. "And we *do* want to do that."

"Right. We wouldn't want Old Agnes to choke on
a dirty ship."

"Old Agnes isn't going to eat anybody."

"You're sure?"

Zelda paused. "Well, *practically.*"

"That gives me a warm, fuzzy feeling of security."

An excited yell came from belowdecks, interrupting the pirates' song for a moment.

"I guess Hilda just found out her magic is back,"
Zelda commented.

"Yeah," Sabrina replied morosely. "Well if you
think she's screaming now, just wait until she finds
out how much point-cleaning is still left to do."

High above *Screamin' Mimi*'s deck, Sabrina stood
in the crow's nest and continued repairing the sailcloth and rigging with her magic. She'd been pointing for hours, following the list Zelda had given her.
Now her finger was so tired that it was shaking, and
she had to steady it with her other hand.

Ropes that tie and ropes that bend,
Knit yourselves and be strong again.

Immediately, the frayed section of rigging she'd
pointed at raveled itself back together and became
like new. She pointed at another section and continued, wishing there was a major spell she could do

121

that would fix the whole ship. Most of the work had been done, and they were now down to spot-pointing.

The sun sat low in the western sky, only minutes away from the beginning of true night. Sabrina wondered where Harvey was, but she knew with the different time zones in the Other Realm that he could still be at Ye Olde Doges in the basset hound suit.

She sighed, spotted another section of rigging that needed repair, and started pointing again. The ropes started shaking even as her magic worked to make them new again. She peered over the side and saw Tommy climbing the rigging toward the crow's nest.

"Hi," Sabrina said brightly. Tommy really was cute, even though the idea that he and Aunt Zelda might once have been close was really creepy. "What brings you up here?"

Tommy easily climbed over the edge of the crow's nest and joined her. "Time for me shift. And I brought ye somethin' to drink, if ye want." He offered a canteen.

"No," Sabrina said. "Thanks." She'd pointed up energy drinks as she'd needed them.

"Ever been at sea before?" Tommy stowed his gear, making the most of the small room, then even managed to somehow drape his lanky frame across the edge of the crow's nest and the ratlines.

"Not like this," Sabrina answered.

"So what do ye do with yerself?"

Briefly, Sabrina explained about Westbridge and going to high school.

When she finished, Tommy only shook his head. "I couldn't manage livin' like that. Goin' to school every day would just be too much."

"It's not every day," Sabrina responded. "It's only five days a week. It just *feels* like every day."

"Me?" Tommy laid back on the ratlines, looking totally cool and comfortable. "Give me the sea and a fair wind to fill me sails. I'll make do."

"How long have you been a sailor?" Sabrina asked.

"A pirate, don't you mean?" Tommy grinned, flashing white teeth.

"Yeah, I guess I do."

Tommy shrugged, rolling his sun-browned shoulders. "Hundreds of years. An' all that time that I been out upon the salt as I have, I still don't truly know this sea. I don't think you can know any sea fully. It keeps a-turnin' over, it does, a-bringin' up stuff from the bottom and a-takin' stuff down from the top. The sea's mystery is what makes her so romantic." He gazed out at the ocean.

Wow, Sabrina thought, *I could probably sit and listen to him talk for a long time.* Then an image of Harvey in the basset hound outfit flashed through her head and made her feel a little guilty. "You've never wanted to be a ship's captain?"

Tommy grinned. "Nah. Bein' cap'n of a ship doesn't look like any kind of fun at all. I'm a-holdin' out for king of the pirates. Now there's a job I'd be fond of. An' what do you want to be when you grow up?"

Sabrina shook her head. "I don't know. I guess I'm not there yet."

"Me neither." Tommy smiled at her again, but this time his grin quickly faded. He pushed himself up from the ratlines and stared out to sea. "We've got troubles."

Sabrina gazed in the direction he was pointing. "What? I don't see anything."

"That there's a ship's sails," Tommy said, taking up the spyglass he'd brought up.

Sabrina extended her own spyglass. She kept both eyes open as she raked the ocean with her gaze and asked Tommy for directions. Then she saw the ship.

It had three masts. From the pirate conversations she'd heard lately, she knew this meant it was a big ship.

"See her colors?" Tommy asked.

Sabrina tracked her spyglass along the ship's side till she reached the flag fluttering from the pole in the stern. The flag showed a silver fisherhawk emblazoned on a field of purple and gray.

"That's one of Queen Becca's ships," Tommy declared worriedly. The gentle breeze ruffled his hair. "They must have figured out where we'd be sailing after we left Governor's Island."

"Are you sure?" Sabrina asked. "What would it be doing here?"

"There ain't but one reason," Tommy explained. "And we're it."

As it turned out, there were actually three ships giving chase. They closed in on *Screamin' Mimi* like sharks cutting through the water, one on each side and one coming up from behind.

Sabrina stood with Zelda, Hilda, and Eddie in the stern. All of them watched grimly as the vessels closed the distance on the pirate ship.

"They're warships," Eddie growled. "*Mimi* ain't a-gonna be able to outrun them."

"Maybe you could summon up stronger winds," Sabrina suggested.

"No," Zelda answered instantly. "The Gentle Sea isn't a place where you can use that kind of magic without some kind of repercussions. The sea is magical in its own right. You can avoid the Gentle Sea, but you can't ignore its rules once you've set sail on it. Try to call up more winds to aid you in an escape, you might get no wind at all or you might get hit by a hurricane."

"You might," Hilda stated, "have let us know that before we came with you."

"One thing's for certain, Cap'n," Eddie said calmly, "they're going to overtake us in just a little while."

"Maybe we still have enough time left." Zelda pointed ahead at the large patch of fog they'd spotted only a few minutes earlier. "If we can make it to the fog before they reach us, we stand a chance."

"We can't let them take us, Cap'n," Eddie said. "If'n they do and we don't get back to King Feargus the Second, why the king will have our lads tortured."

"I know."

Glancing amidships, Sabrina watched the flurry of activity as the cannon gunnery crews got their weapons ready. They filled the cannon with powder and rammed cannonballs down the muzzles, standing by expectantly.

"We're going to fight three ships? That's crazy." Salem perched on the stern railing and looked down at the artillery crews. He'd spent the afternoon fishing, trying to catch one of the magnificent swordfish that swam nearby in schools. "Even back in the day, when I was a pirate captain, I never took on more than two."

"Did you win?" Sabrina asked nervously. It was one thing to watch an occasional pirate movie with Errol Flynn or a movie about Horatio Hornblower with Ioan Gruffudd, who was a definite hottie, but it was another thing to think of actual ship-to-ship fighting.

"Most of the time," Salem said. "Boy I hated losing."

Eddie drew his cutlass. "Another few minutes, Cap'n, and they're a-gonna be alongside us. They'll bring their main batteries to bear and blow us to pieces."

"No," Zelda said. "They want us alive."

"They blew up the caves back in Governor's Island," Sabrina reminded her.

"Only after they got frustrated with trying to find us."

"If an enemy wants you alive," Salem wailed, "that's even worse. They'll just play with you, wear you down, chew on your ears . . ." He paused. "No, wait. Those are my instincts coming through now."

Small clouds of smoke suddenly jetted from the side of the ship on the left. A rolling crackle of thunder followed, echoing over the water.

"They're a-firin' at us!" Eddie declared.

Chapter 10

The cannonballs screamed through the air with dulled *wooo-wooo-wooo* noises that surprised Sabrina. She hadn't expected them to make any noise at all.

"Get down!" Zelda ordered, catching the teen witch's wrist and pulling her to shelter behind the stern railing. Loud smacks echoed hollowly immediately after, triggering shivers that ran through *Screamin' Mimi.*

"We've been hit!" Salem shrilled. "We've been hit! Man the lifeboats! Get cats and children to safety first!"

Sabrina suddenly got an image of the pirate ship going down, made all too real by the movie *Titanic* Harvey had taken her to.

"Cap'n?" Eddie waited expectantly. "Can we return fire?"

"Only as a last recourse," Zelda replied grimly as

she pushed herself up. "It'll take their crews a little bit to reload. I intend to make the most of that time."

Sabrina stood up, too, and leaned over the railing to see how badly the ship was damaged. Surprisingly, the cannonballs had left only scratches, and none of them had broken through. "What happened to the cannonballs?" she asked.

"They bounced from the hull," Eddie answered. "Wood is naturally tough when it's been treated proper. If'n they get any cannonballs up in the riggin', we're a-gonna have problems because they'll tear the sails and shear the masts. If'n that happens, we'll be a sittin' duck."

Zelda pointed at the first ship and recited,

Ship at sea
In the midst of a fight,
Cork up the cannon
And do it right!

The crew aboard Queen Becca's ship shouted in surprise as huge corks suddenly filled the cannon muzzles. Turning quickly, Zelda stoppered the other ships' cannons as well. However, it didn't stop the ships from closing in. The sailors hurled hoarse, angry shouts after them.

"Okay," Salem said nervously, "this is good. We've been hit, but we aren't sinking."

"I don't think they was a-tryin' to hurt us," Eddie said. "I think they're a-wantin' us alive an' in one piece."

"Alive is good," Salem stated. He rested his front paws on the railing and peered over the side.

"They want ye alive, Whiskers, so they can torture ye at their leisure. Queen Becca has her own dungeons."

"Okay," Salem said, "rethinking that escape is definitely preferable."

Sabrina glanced ahead, noticing that the fog was a lot closer to *Screamin' Mimi*'s prow now. But was it close enough? The three warships closed in, and the ships' crews brandished swords and pistols.

"Artillery commanders," Zelda called out in a strong voice, "stand ready to fire."

Sabrina stared at her aunt in disbelief. "You're going to shoot at them?"

"They was a-shootin' at us," Eddie pointed out, "an' didn't seem to have no qualms about it."

"But—but—but—" Sabrina stuttered. "You can't just shoot someone."

"Aye, an' ye're right about that, girlie," the big pirate said. "Takes a bit of luck, it does. A-timin' the ocean's rise and fall of yerself and them others can be vexin'."

"Aunt Zelda," Sabrina protested.

"Not now, Sabrina," her aunt responded. She addressed the gunnery crews. "I want their masts cut from their decks. I don't want any of those people hurt if we can help it."

"Aye, Cap'n!" the artillery commanders called back.

"Stand by to fire," Zelda ordered.

"Standing by."

Sabrina stood frozen by the railing. She didn't want to watch, but she couldn't help herself. *And Zelda wasn't wanting me to involve myself in Harvey's problem at the mall?* At the same time she was thinking how lucky Gerry and his friends may have been that Black Eddie Peas had arrived.

Screamin' Mimi rolled up the next wave, giving her a clear view of all three ships pursuing her.

"Fire!" Zelda commanded.

Immediately, all sounds were drowned in rumbling thunder from the cannon. Thick, black smoke swirled over the deck.

Sabrina's nose burned from the acrid stench. Terrified, she watched as the cannonballs struck the first ship. In seconds, some of the rigging, sails, and the stern mast ripped apart and tumbled down. The ship's crew dodged quickly out of the way, and none were hurt. The loss of sails caused the ship to slow immediately. When Sabrina glanced around, she noticed that the other two ships had been damaged as well.

"Woo-hoo!" Sabrina yelped in excited relief. All three ships started to fall back.

Screamin' Mimi surged ahead, falling down the next wave, then climbing the one after that. Misty fog swirled around Sabrina, leaving damp places on her face and hands. *We're going to get away!*

Zelda gave orders to reload the cannon as the pirate ship sailed into the fogbank. In a few seconds, the fog was thick enough that their pursuers couldn't be seen.

The moment after that, however, Tommy cried out from the crow's nest. " 'Ware ahead! 'Ware ahead! There's a ship dead ahead!"

Sabrina glanced forward in time to see the huge ship ahead of them. Dozens of men lined the railing, all of them fisting weapons.

"It was a trap!" Salem squealed.

"Hard to port!" Zelda ordered.

The helmsman yanked on the big steering wheel to turn the rudder, but Sabrina knew they'd never make the turn. *Screamin' Mimi* banged up against the other ship. The hollow *boom* of the hulls slamming together penetrated even the cottony feeling in Sabrina's ears that had been left by the cannon blasts.

The impact knocked everyone from their feet. Sabrina tried to push herself up as Zelda shouted orders and tried to get her crew organized.

But it was too late. The crew from the new ship threw grappling lines, which hooked onto *Screamin' Mimi*'s railing. Then the sailors from the big ship slid down the ropes or jumped into the pirate ship's rigging from their higher decks.

Sabrina had to dodge out of the way to keep the new arrivals from landing on her. One of the sailors stepped on Salem's tail, and the cat cried out in alarm. Sabrina ran to Salem and quickly picked him up.

The sailors held their weapons at the ready, circling *Screamin' Mimi*'s crew. A big man in a red-and-white striped shirt approached Zelda. He fisted a cutlass in one hand. "In the name of Her Sovereign Majesty Queen Becca, I demand your surrender, Cap'n Zellie."

They know her name, Sabrina realized. She thought quickly, struggling to think of a spell that would help them. *Maybe a stop-time spell.* But then what would they do with all the sailors? She felt confused and more than a little concerned.

Zelda lifted her arm to point.

The big man in the striped shirt pointed first.

Immediately, an anti-pointing Club formed on Zelda's arm, preventing her from using her magic.

He's a warlock, Sabrina realized.

The big man smiled, but it wasn't friendly. "We can do this easy or hard, but you're coming with me. So what's it going to be?"

"I'm too young to torture," Salem cried, whimpering loudly. "Someone call the SPCA."

"Control yourself, Salem," Hilda suggested. "You're only making matters worse."

"How am I making matters worse?" Salem asked. "We're all going to be tortured in Queen Becca's dungeons, and then we're going to die!"

"You're making matters worse with all that whining," Zelda said irritably. "That's torture enough."

Sabrina looked at the anti-pointing Club on her arm. The guy in the striped shirt was named Chatterly, and his magic was really strong, because the anti-point Club spell wasn't easy to do. Of course, it helped that he'd been prepared to use it.

Salem continued whining and crying as they were escorted into the ship's hold.

"Someone get a muzzle for the cat," Chatterly said as he walked beside the witches.

"You're not muzzling my cat," Sabrina said.

Chatterly glanced at her. "And get a gag for the girl if she isn't quiet."

"You're not gagging my niece," Hilda said.

Chatterly raised his eyebrows. "Gags all the way around if you wish."

Angrily, Sabrina stayed quiet, grateful that Salem got control of himself enough to stop whimpering. Big tears still rolled down the cat's face. Sabrina wished she could offer some hope, but things definitely looked bad.

After they'd surrendered on *Screamin' Mimi*, they'd been taken aboard Queen Becca's flagship, *Victory*. The flagship turned out to be a floating palace, complete with queen's chambers and a portable dungeon.

Sabrina stepped through the double doorway ahead and into a large room. Torches burned on the walls, aiding the natural light that streamed in through the windows at the top of the room. Thick carpet covered the floor. Paintings and colorful vases were on display.

A beautiful woman with red-gold hair and a milky complexion sat in a throne on a raised dais at the other end of the room. Three portraits of the woman—one in a garden, another on a castle wall, and a third in armor on a battlefield—occupied the wall behind her. She wore a beautiful emerald green dress shimmering with sequins.

The queen's guard escorted Sabrina, her aunts, Salem, Eddie, and Abner before Queen Becca. The rest of *Screamin' Mimi*'s crew remained under guard aboard ship.

"These are the fugitives we've been searching for, Captain Chatterly?" the queen asked.

"Aye, Your Majesty," Chatterly responded.

"Which of you leads this motley crew?" Queen Becca asked.

"I do," Zelda answered.

"And you seek the treasure that Captain Cutter stole from King Feargus three hundred and more years ago?"

"No," Zelda said. "We were on a fishing expedition. Just a three-hour tour."

Queen Becca glared at her coldly. "We are not amused."

"Oh good," Zelda replied, "the feeling is mutual. Now, if you'll let us go, we'll all be happier."

"Silence!" Queen Becca roared sharply. She pressed her hands together before her. "We seek that treasure also."

Sabrina felt panicky. They were there to find the lost treasure to free the men King Feargus the Second was holding. If Queen Becca got it, Sabrina was sure the Ootnannian king would never see it.

"I don't know where it is," Zelda replied.

The queen arched her eyebrows. "No, but you must have some idea or you wouldn't be here. According to Chatterly, you live with your sister and niece in the mortal realm."

Somebody, Sabrina thought, *has a big mouth.*

"We've been searching for you ever since you escaped Governor's Island," the queen said. "We want to know where you're headed."

Zelda hesitated for only a moment. "To the Sargasso of Lost Ships."

Queen Becca's eyes widened in surprise. "Why?"

"Because that's where we believe Captain Cutter is." Zelda briefly explained about the captain's disappearance.

"And you expect to find him alive?"

"I really don't think Old Agnes has eaten anyone in centuries," Zelda said.

"We don't think you know as much about sea monsters in this realm as you believe you do."

Sabrina remembered the near miss the elasmosaurus had made against Salem and thought maybe the queen was right. Zelda had been gone from the area for over three hundred years.

The queen leaned forward in anticipation. "But if Captain Cutter still lives within Old Agnes's belly, he would be able to tell you where the treasure is."

"Whether he actually would remains to be seen," Zelda said. "We were planning to ask. That appears to have been interrupted."

The queen was silent for a moment, obviously thinking. "Only delayed. One of you shall still make the voyage to the Sargasso of Lost Ships." She glanced at Sabrina. "And we choose you."

"Me?" Sabrina couldn't believe it. "You can't send me! I mean, you don't want to send me! I probably know the least of what's going on here."

"Exactly." The queen smiled. "That idea pleases us. If old Agnes's appetite turns out to be more . . . *rapacious* than your aunt believes, I will still have her and her sister to assist me." She smiled again. "Actually, this idea pleases us even more as we think about it."

"Trust me," Sabrina said. "Sending me to take care of something important really doesn't always work out for the best. I mean, I've goofed up some really important things, and from the sound of this, finding that treasure is really important."

"Our mind is made up," Queen Becca stated crossly. "If you argue with us, you will only upset us."

"Sabrina's going to need someone to help her," Salem said. Everyone turned to look at the cat.

"Who let this wretched creature on our ship?" the queen demanded.

"Not wretched," Salem said, flicking his tail

proudly. "I'm an American shorthair, a truly magnificent example of the breed."

"We hate cat dander," Queen Becca declared. "Chatterly, you will be punished for your oversight."

"My queen," Chatterly said, "the cat is not what he appears to be. He was once a warlock named Salem Saberhagen."

"The warlock who almost took over the mortal realm?" The queen gazed at Salem with fascination.

"Aye," Chatterly said.

Salem preened proudly.

"Were you not in your present condition," Queen Becca said, "we might be interested in getting to know you better. But cat dander definitely offends our royal sinuses." She sneezed for effect. "Captain Chatterly, make sure the little beast accompanies the pirate ship."

"Aye, my queen."

"But I'm really not much of a monster hunter," Sabrina blurted.

Queen Becca waved the complaint off casually. "You will do until we find we have need of another." She held her arm out.

A large parrot with bright green feathers and a red-and-yellow face flew down from one of the windows and landed on the queen's arm. The parrot cocked its head and glared at Salem with one hostile black eye.

"Nahsty little creature, 'e is," the parrot squawked in a Cockney accent, flapping its wings.

"Don't get ideas that you can run off or fool us," Queen Becca said. "We shall have our eyes upon you the whole time. We present to you Captain Polly Swabbucket, who shall accompany you on your quest."

The parrot extended her wings in a deep curtsy. " 'Ere now, and mind you listen at me closely. I'll not be after 'avin' no foolishness on any watch o'mine. I'll 'ave your guts for garters, I will."

Salem hissed.

The queen's eyes hardened. "We shall not entertain any further delays. Is that understood?"

Sabrina looked at her aunts.

"We'll be alright," Hilda said, offering a supportive smile.

"Do what you have to do, honey," Zelda told her. "Find Captain Cutter. He was always a smart man. Maybe he can help."

"There will be no help," Queen Becca said coldly. "If you challenge us or our royal command, you will only be asking for disaster."

With a heavy heart, Sabrina watched as *Screamin' Mimi* got her head in the wind and pulled away from Queen Becca's flagship. The magical fog Chatterly had hidden the ship in was gone, and she had a clear view of the vessel. It was easily five or six times as large as the pirate ship.

Sabrina glanced down at the anti-pointing Club that remained on her arm. Chatterly had told her it would disappear the instant she was out of pointing range of the royal flagship. He also told her that as soon as she got within pointing range of the queen again, it would reappear.

"There, there, girlie," Black Eddie Peas said, patting her on the shoulder. "Everythin's a-gonna be all right."

Sabrina's eyes burned, and she barely restrained her tears. Things felt really hopeless. She could return to the mortal realm, but not without her aunts.

"What makes you think everything's going to be all right?" she asked, regretting the anger in her voice.

Eddie smiled with a little surprise. "Why, girlie, it always has been before."

"Except for the part about Old Agnes eating Captain Cutter."

The big pirate rubbed the back of his neck in embarrassment. "Aye, an' ye got me there. That were truly an uncommon surprise."

"You might want to think about it," Sabrina said, listening to the familiar creak of the rigging as the sails strained against the wind. She tried to pretend everything was normal, but it didn't feel that way. "Captain Cutter might have company before very much longer."

"Aye, an' that's right enough, I guess. Never really considered meself as a victual. That thought might take some getting used to."

Sabrina stood at the railing till the distance grew

too great to see the flagship. A final wave took *Screamin' Mimi* up over a watery horizon, and when the ship settled down again, only the expanse of gray-green sea was left.

Sabrina figured she felt as lonely in that moment as she ever had.

" 'Ere now," Polly Swabbucket complained, flapping her great wings, "an' see, you're gonna 'ave to get an 'andle on that flea-bitten cat o' yours."

Sabrina stood at the stern railing and stared wearily at the parrot. Over the last two days, Salem and Polly had constantly been at each other's throats—literally. The teen witch had reached her breaking point.

"He's not flea-bitten," Sabrina said. "Back home he's given his baths regularly." *Under protest as always, but that's beside the point.*

Polly squawked irritably and waved her wings. "Now you've got a poor attitude, you do."

"Tough," Sabrina said. "It comes with being blackmailed into hunting sea monsters for greedy queens."

The parrot cocked her head and turned a beady eye on her. "An' should I report back to good Queen Becca that you've been disparagin' 'er?"

Sabrina smiled. "Then I see a pot of dumplings in your future as soon as I get my pointing finger limbered up."

Polly shook all over, her feathers sticking out

everywhere. "You've got an ill temper for one so young."

"You think?"

"Did someone mention dumplings?" Salem bounded up onto the railing quickly, just out of reach of Polly's claws and wings, but he succeeded in startling the parrot all the same. He stared at the ungainly looking bird and licked his chops. "I have to admit, parrot and dumplings had somehow escaped my list, but it would go nicely with parrot pie or with a nice ginger-pear chutney."

Polly pointed a wing at Salem. " 'E's been torturin' me, 'e 'as. Always writing down recipes about birdfolk, particularly parrots."

"You'd be surprised," Salem said, "how many uses there are for them. I know I was."

"Salem's only getting back at you for the things you've been doing to him," Sabrina said.

"But I'm entitled," Polly squawked indignantly. "I'm Her Majesty's royal spy."

Sabrina sighed. Things had gone from worse to worser. Maybe it wasn't grammatically correct, but it sure suited how she felt. And somehow she felt certain that things hadn't gotten as bad as they could.

The Sargasso of Lost Ships wasn't where Aunt Zelda had believed it was. After they'd reached the area marked on the map, they'd started sailing in ever-widening circles in the hopes of finding it somewhere.

"Look, both of you," Sabrina said angrily, ticking off points on her fingers. "I've really got other things on my mind. Hilda and Zelda are in a lot of trouble. The crew of this ship is stripped down to barely enough people to keep us going. The rest of that crew is split between a king and queen who don't really like each other. The Sargasso of Lost Ships should be renamed the Lost Sargasso of Lost Ships. And I'm not sure how the time measures up against time in the mortal realm. I could have stood Harvey up for a date by now, which really wouldn't make me happy." She stopped and drew in a deep breath, all of her fingers extended on her hand. "And I can't add your problems with each other in there because I'm all out of fingers."

"Touchy, touchy," Polly commented.

"Moody," Salem corrected. "Definitely moody. I've seen her like this before."

Sabrina pointed in their direction. Tiny ball and chains formed around their feet. "Stay," she said and walked away. "Any time you come close to me, those ball and chains will reappear."

" 'Ere now," Polly objected. "This 'ere is 'ardly cricket. An' I'm of a mind to—"

Another quick point put muzzles on both animals.

"And the muzzles." Sabrina turned and walked amidships. She took a brief moment of pride in how *Screamin' Mimi* looked. Between the crew's efforts and her magic, the ship had stayed, well, *shipshape*.

She climbed the rigging, managing it much easier now that she'd gotten more practiced at it.

Tommy was in the crow's nest eating a cheese sandwich. At least with her magic working, they'd all been eating well.

Fattening up for Old Agnes, she couldn't help thinking.

"Anything?" she asked as she stepped into the crow's nest.

Tommy shook his head. "Nothin', Cap'n. Sorry." All the crew had taken to calling her Captain, following Eddie's lead and maybe his command.

Sabrina looked out to sea, wishing she knew of some way to find the Sargasso. Eddie, Tommy, and Abner, who were all allowed to come with her, had checked the maps and agreed that they'd arrived at the right spot.

The Sargasso just hadn't been there.

She'd considered trying to get hold of her father or the Witches' Council, but none of them would have been able to do anything against the Shield of the Amazing Bob. And if there was one thing Sabrina had learned in high school, it was that giving the appearance of doing what she was told was generally the best thing.

She desperately hoped that after she found the Sargasso of Lost Ships and Old Agnes she'd have a positively brilliant idea.

"Hey," Tommy said, interrupting her thoughts, "it looks like yer cat's in trouble." He pointed.

Sabrina glanced down, not believing it when she spotted Cap'n Polly hopping at Salem with a short sword clutched tightly in one foot. Salem backed up, yowling and spitting now, barely avoiding the sword. In seconds, the parrot had Salem backing out onto a plank, forcing the cat over the gray-green sea.

"Hey!" Sabrina yelled, leaning over the edge of the crow's nest. "You two knock that off! Don't make me come down there! I'll turn this ship right around and—"

Without warning, a long, dark purple tentacle snaked up from the sea and reached for Salem!

Chapter 11

☆

"**S**alem!" Sabrina shrieked as the purple tentacle oozed along the gangplank toward the cat. The tentacle moved like a gigantic tongue and tracked slime over the gangplank.

"I've got him," Tommy said. He threw himself out of the crow's nest and onto the nearest sail.

Worried about Salem and used to moving around in the rigging now, Sabrina followed the young pirate. She hit the sailcloth and thought for a moment it wasn't going to hold her. Then the material stretched tight, and Sabrina slid down the slope of the belled sail, gaining speed.

Cap'n Polly had spotted the searching tentacle now, and she dropped the short sword she held in one clawed foot. She hopped into the air and flew away.

Salem sat and preened, unaware of what was behind him. "I guess I showed her. There's not a bird alive that can take Salem Saberhagen in a fair—"

The tentacle tapped Salem's tail. The cat turned around, and Sabrina saw his eyes get really wide.

"Yow!" Salem screamed. He dug his claws into the gangplank and tried to run, but the tentacle wrapped around his tail. "Somebody save me! Help!"

Tommy slid from the sail and landed on the deck. Sabrina landed only a heartbeat behind the young pirate. The rest of the ship's crew stayed back, afraid of the great sea monster reaching up from the depths.

Fearlessly, Tommy dashed out onto the gangplank. He grabbed a belaying pin from the railing. The belaying pin looked like a rolling pin, but it was mostly used by sailors to tie and secure ropes, and as a weapon to batter enemies.

The young pirate grabbed Salem by the scruff of the neck, then whacked the tentacle with the belaying pin. The tentacle pulled back immediately. Tommy turned and ran back toward the deck.

Just as Tommy reached the ship's side, a giant squid at least forty feet long broke the surface of the sea. Deep purple, leathery skin covered the bulbous head. It flailed all eight tentacles, grabbing hold of the ship's railing and snapping the gangplank off.

Sabrina grabbed the front of Tommy's shirt and pulled him aboard before he could fall into the sea. *Screamin' Mimi* rocked back and forth as the great monster fought to yank the ship down.

Eddie joined Sabrina, yelling loudly over the frightened cries of the crew. He braced himself against the railing, one of his pistols in his hand. "Ye've got to do somethin', Cap'n! If'n ye don't, that yonder thing's a-gonna shake ol' *Mimi* apart, then snap us up outta the brine at its leisure!"

Sabrina pointed at the giant squid.

*Here we are with luck
That's only gone to pot.
But here's a spell
That can really tie the knot.*

Abruptly, the squid's tentacles tore free of the ship's railing. Writhing like snakes, they tied two by two into immense bow ties. Constrained by its own body, the squid flailed and thrashed, and quickly sank from sight.

Sabrina took a shaky breath as she peered over the side. She took Salem from Tommy. "Was that Old Agnes?"

"Oh no," Eddie replied. "Ol' Agnes, ye see, now she's a big 'un."

Speechless, Sabrina stared at Eddie. Finally, she found her voice and croaked, "Bigger than that?"

Eddie nodded. "Aye. Probably five or six times that one's size." He paused, eyeing the sea. "But we must be gettin' close. Squids that size usually hang around Ol' Agnes."

"Is that good news or bad news?" Sabrina asked.

"Well, ye wanted to find Ol' Agnes," Eddie said. "Ye're about to get yer chance."

Four hours later, under the mid-afternoon sun burning down on the Gentle Sea, Sabrina stared out at the Sargasso of Lost Ships. She'd ordered *Screamin' Mimi* to a full stop a good distance out from the floating wreckage of ravaged ships.

From the crow's nest, she surveyed the ships through her spyglass. Eddie, Tommy, and Abner all crowded in the small platform with her.

The Sargasso of Lost Ships was aptly named. Sabrina guessed that there were over a hundred vessels grouped together into a floating wooden island. The ships showed a lot of damage; some of them were only pieces of ships. The ships were all overturned or upside down. What was left of the sails and rigging dragged through the water. Through the spyglass, she saw something that really surprised her.

"There are people living on those ships," she gasped, spotting the tiny figures among the wrecks.

"Aye," Eddie said. "Them what was unlucky enough to get away in time got stuck on them ships. We've heard stories about the like before. Ol' Agnes's survivors fish and live off what they can catch and scavenge from the wrecked ships. Usually they can make it through enough years that Ol'

Agnes moves on and leaves 'em so they can be rescued."

"Aunt Zelda said it would probably be fifty years before Old Agnes's eggs hatch."

The big pirate scratched his chin. "That sounds about right."

Sabrina sighed and put her spyglass away. "We don't have fifty years to wait." *If I haven't missed Harvey's date by now, I'd definitely miss it waiting around for that.*

"Aye," Eddie agreed. "So I guess we've got nothin' left except the gettin' to it."

"Right," Sabrina said, trying not to think that sailing *Screamin' Mimi* into the Sargasso of Lost Ships was a lot like sending Ol' Agnes a snack tray loaded with hors d'oeuvres.

"Ahoy! Ahoy the ship there! Have you come to rescue us?"

Sabrina studied the men, women, and children lining the broken ships at the side of the Sargasso. She guessed there were at least a hundred of them, with more coming. They'd obviously been there a long time. Walkways made of rope and pieces of wood hung between the various ships, linking them like city streets.

"Have you come to rescue us?" a heavyset man demanded again. The other people echoed his words.

"Spokesman," Eddie grunted. "Ye realize, of course, that this lot is panicked and could be some trouble?"

"Yes," Sabrina replied. *Why does this have to be so complicated?* She peered down into the water, seeking some sign of Old Agnes but not really wanting to find it.

"You can't stay here very long," the man called from the shipwrecks. He raced along the broken vessels, trying to keep pace with the pirate ship. "Old Agnes will be up and about soon for her evening feeding, and then she'll destroy your ship as well. I know you can't take all of us away from here, but take the ones that you can."

Listening to the man nearly broke Sabrina's heart, but she focused on what he'd said. "When's feeding time?"

"Ye realize, of course, that Ol' Agnes might not exactly listen to reason," Eddie said. "I feel that I got to point that out to you."

"I know," Sabrina responded. She gazed down into the ocean depths, waiting, her heart banging away at the back of her throat.

She'd kept *Screamin' Mimi* far enough away from the collection of broken ships that the people marooned there didn't try to swim out. Besides Old Agnes, it seemed that sharks liked to cruise through the area to pick up snacks as well.

In order to keep Old Agnes from eating any more of the survivors on the shipwrecks, they had to fish every day. They hung their catches in a big net on the north side of the Sargasso. The sea monster ate twice a day, once in the morning and again in the evening. If there wasn't enough food, Old Agnes would eat one or more of the survivors. She conserved her energy while keeping her eggs warm. She'd created the Sargasso and trapped victims so she wouldn't have to hunt.

The Sargasso spokesman, Fred Derf, said they knew the sea monster didn't really eat the survivors because they could still hear them yelling to be freed from Old Agnes's gullet. Still, the belly of a sea monster wasn't believed to be a very comfortable place.

Suddenly, the water between *Screamin' Mimi* and the Sargasso started roiling. Great circles spread out from a central point, smashing waves. Then a great shadow showed up against the gray-green depths, coming steadily closer to the surface.

Sabrina's breath froze in her throat as more of the giant sea serpent took shape. Old Agnes's head was more than fifty feet across. Ridged fins stuck out from her forehead like eyebrows. Other fins gave her the appearance of having ears and an unruly beard. Her skin was a rainbow of greens that scintillated like chain mail.

Old Agnes surfaced, somehow looking tired. She opened her great maw, and the spokesman gave the command to release the catch. The net handlers yanked, spilling the contents. Hundreds of shiny fish dropped down into the waiting serpent's maw with rapid, smacking *plops*.

While the sea monster noisily ate, the people trapped in her stomach screamed for help.

"Now what?" Eddie asked softly, looking hypnotized by the sheer immensity of the sea serpent.

"I don't know," Sabrina admitted. "I was hoping for some kind of idea."

"Runnin' sounds good to me."

Abruptly, Old Agnes switched her gaze toward the pirate ship, drawn by their voices or by some magical sense. Her great, black eyes surveyed the ship.

"You're new," the sea monster said in a low, rumbling voice. She cocked her head and slid closer. "New is interesting." She paused. "New is also dangerous."

"I really don't like that look," Salem said. "It's like she's reading the menu."

Sabrina suddenly realized how exposed she was on *Screamin' Mimi*'s deck. But she needed to be close to figure out what she was going to do with the sea monster.

Almost effortlessly, Old Agnes lunged at the pirate ship. The sea monster seized Sabrina, Salem, Cap'n Polly, and Eddie with her lips, carefully avoiding them with her teeth.

Sabrina struggled against the giant lips but couldn't free herself. She heard Salem and Cap'n Polly squalling in fear, but she couldn't reach them either.

In the next minute, the teen witch was flipped high into the air. She saw the Gentle Sea and the Sargasso of Lost Ships spread out around her, the afternoon sun fading in the west, and the gigantic sea serpent beneath her.

Then Old Agnes gulped Sabrina down, and everything turned black.

"Oh woe is me," Salem bawled. "It's bad enough I was turned into a cat, but now I'm monster kibble. It's just so unfair." He cried some more.

Sabrina had to struggle to pull her face from a sticky surface. When she pointed up a small flashlight, she discovered that the sticky surface was Old Agnes's gigantic pink tongue. In the next instant, the sea serpent swallowed again, and the tongue shot along like an amusement park ride.

Hanging on to her flashlight, Sabrina landed with a wet thud that knocked the breath from her. She sat up and shined the light around her, discovering that she was in a huge, pink cavern.

Not a cavern, she corrected. *Old Agnes's stomach*. Salem was still crying nearby. She sat up and looked for her cat and found him lying in a puddle of liquid that remained unidentified for a moment. Then she realized what it was. *Ew! Monster spit! Gross!*

"Hey," someone said. "She has a magic light."

Sabrina realized that a flashlight didn't fit in with this part of the Other Realm, but it felt comforting. She heard footsteps sloshing closer to her and widened the beam. When she shone it up at the top of the sea monster's gullet, it filled the area with a soft incandescence.

At least a dozen people were in Old Agnes's stomach with her. Eight of them were men, and three of them were women. The twelfth member was a little boy that looked like he'd been carved of cherrywood.

"Um, hello," Sabrina said self-consciously. *What do you say to someone you meet in a sea monster's stomach? Nice indigestion we're having?* "My name is Sabrina Spellman. None of you know me."

The lost looks on their faces confirmed that. The flashlight fascinated most of them.

"I'm looking for Captain Cutter of *Screamin' Mimi*," Sabrina said hopefully.

"Aye. That'd be me, young miss." A grizzled old man stepped from the shadows into the flashlight glow. Wiry gray hair poked everywhere in disarray, long enough to tangle in his beard. "An' who are ye?"

Eddie stepped up to meet the older man, a huge grin on his face. "She's Zellie's niece." He took Captain Cutter's hand and pulled him into a bear hug. "Ah, an' it's good to see ye again, Cap'n. I thought ye lost and gone forever."

A look of astonishment covered the old captain's face. "Zellie's here?"

"Surely ye didn't think I was a-gonna let ye rot here forever?" Eddie said.

"Right," Salem said sarcastically. "You only let him rot here for the last twenty years or so."

"Twenty years?" Captain Cutter repeated. "Has it really been that long?"

"Yes," Sabrina answered.

Sadness touched the captain's blue eyes. "What of me ship then, Eddie? Tell me about *Screamin' Mimi.*"

"We really don't have time for old home week," Salem grumbled. "If Old Agnes makes one good swallow—or even a hiccup—we're all history."

Sabrina prodded the side of Old Agnes's gullet with a piece of driftwood she'd found. Unfortunately, the sea monster had no reaction at all. Sabrina had been keeping up with—and correcting—Eddie's version of how they'd arrived at the Sargasso of Lost Ships. Captain Cutter had only a few questions, and Sabrina got the sense that he was a man of action.

"Have you ever tried tickling her before?" Sabrina asked. "Sometimes if you get tickled too much it can make you throw up." She paused, thinking about it. "Not that throwing up would be all that great of a thing, but at least we'd be out."

"Yes," a dozen of the other captives answered irritably. They sat around on chairs they'd fashioned from driftwood and broken pieces of ship that had remained in Old Agnes's gullet. "She's not ticklish."

"Oh." *You don't have to be so snippy,* Sabrina thought. *It was only a suggestion.* It was obvious that the other captives had given up any thought of rescue a long time ago.

In truth, the teen witch was also getting doubtful about any form of escape. Locked within the sea monster's gullet, her magic didn't work. Captain

Cutter had suggested that her spells failed because Old Agnes herself was magical in nature.

"Zellie did come a-lookin' for Feargus the Second's treasure that we took all them years ago?" Captain Cutter asked Sabrina after Eddie had finished.

"Yes," Sabrina answered.

"She wanted to give it to Feargus the Second?"

"To get your crew back, sure." Frustrated, Sabrina dropped the piece of wood.

"Does Zellie know what that treasure is?" Captain Cutter asked.

"No." Sabrina couldn't believe people weren't more interested in trying to get away from the sea monster. They sat numbly, almost bored. *Okay, so maybe escape is hard, but it can't be impossible.*

"Now that I know what that treasure holds," Captain Cutter said, "I know why Feargus the Second wants it back."

That caught Sabrina's attention. "Why?"

"Ye know the Shield of the Amazing Bob prevents any witch or warlock or faerie person from working spells on Ootnanni, Governor's Island, the Queen's Island, and a few scattered others."

Sabrina nodded.

"Well, according to what I've been able to cipher out about this thing"—from around his neck Captain Cutter took a leather pouch on a string—"it gives a witch protection from the shield." He took an object from the pouch.

"That's so pretty." Sabrina gazed at the necklace

Captain Cutter held. The thin gold chain held a bright purple stone that sparkled even in the dimness of Old Agnes's stomach. Then she spotted the cameo of a severe-faced woman inset in the stone. "Whoa! Now there's someone in desperate need of an Oprah makeover!"

The woman in the cameo looked like she was really mad. Her eyebrows stuck out like toothbrushes, and her mouth was puckered like she'd just bitten into a lemon.

"That's the Amazing Bob's mother," Captain Cutter said.

"How do you know this?" Sabrina asked.

"There was a book that came with the necklace," the captain said, handing Sabrina the necklace.

Sabrina felt a tingle of electricity as she took it. "The Amazing Bob created a talisman that would defeat his own shield?"

"Aye, but he didn't intend to do so. That there ye're a-holdin' in yer hand, that was supposed to be a birthday minder. He was always forgettin' his mother's birthday, so he created that to remind him."

"That explains the picture."

"The necklace didn't work as a birthday minder," Captain Cutter said, "but it did allow witches to use their powers within the shield's effects."

"Oh, this is so cool," Sabrina said. "Maybe I can point us out of Old Agnes's stomach." She tried but only got the *sproing!* of a failed spell. "Okay, we knew it couldn't be that easy. Was there anything else in the treasure chest?"

"No. Just some gold and silver, an' a few trinkets that fetched a fair price here an' there. None of 'em was magical." Captain Cutter nodded at the necklace. "What ye're a-holdin' in yer hand there, that was what both the Kings Feargus was afraid of."

"Only we can't use it because we're inside Old Agnes." Frustrated even more, Sabrina thought quickly. She remembered a cartoon she'd watched as a girl. Excitedly, she picked up some driftwood from the pink stomach. "We could start a fire. If we could get enough smoke in here, maybe Old Agnes would spit us out."

The little wooden boy sitting on the other side of the stomach shook his knotty head. "Nope. We already tried that. Old Agnes just breathes the smoke out. But you can cook the fish that way instead of eating them raw."

"Terrific." Sabrina dropped the wood. "But it just wouldn't be the same without marshmallows. What are we going to do?"

"Well, Cap'n," Eddie spoke up, "when things get tough goin' against pirates, usually we just sing. In fact, there's a nice little ditty that I think would just suit this occasion."

"No," Sabrina said hurriedly. *If I have to hear one more stanza of* "Ninety-Nine Bottles of Ale on the Wall" *I'm going to be sick.*

Eddie looked disappointed.

"Maybe later," Sabrina promised.

"Ahem. Perhaps I 'ave an idea."

Sabrina turned to Cap'n Polly, who perched on a really icky stomach ridge. The parrot didn't look happy and kept shifting from one foot to the other. "You? The queen's spy? You want to help us?"

"Actually, I want to help myself," the parrot corrected, "but if it 'appens to save us all, I can't really be blamed, now can I?"

"I wouldn't think so," Captain Cutter agreed.

"Ah, me 'earties," Cap'n Polly squawked, "we've got a secret weapon Ol' Agnes ain't thought about, we do. 'Ere and there, I've been, sailing all over the Gentle Sea, an' I've never found anythin' so foul as quite matches a cat."

"Now that's a personal opinion I'd call suspect," Salem said.

"Look," Sabrina said sharply. "I know the two of you have personality problems—"

"Aye," Cap'n Polly replied, "we do. But it's not 'is bloomin' personality, or lack thereof, I be speakin' about. It's 'is fur. Never nothin' so bloomin' foul as a cat's dander. 'Course, we're a-gonna have to walk up out of Ol' Agnes's gullet till we find her nasal passages to see if we can't aggravate them."

"Nasal passages? Ew!" Sabrina almost gagged.

"The bird does have a point," Captain Cutter admitted.

"I know," Sabrina complained. "It's all just too icky. Ew, ew, ew!"

"Time's a-wastin' if'n you want to rescue Zellie and Hillie," Captain Cutter reminded her.

"I know," Sabrina replied, "but I want you all to know I'm going under protest."

Old Agnes had two nasal passages, and both of them were as big as garages. Both of them were also clamped shut against the ocean.

Sabrina shined her flashlight over them. She stood on the slippery pink roof of the sea monster's mouth and tried not to think about what she was stepping in. "Okay, now what?"

"Now we gotta make Ol' Agnes sneeze," Captain Cutter said. Despite their doubts about whether the scheme would work, the other captives had followed and stood behind them.

Sabrina held Salem out at arm's reach and shook him. *Surely there will be enough cat dander from this.*

Salem's head wobbled back and forth. He fought against her. "Hey, hey, hey! Watch the fu-fu-fu-fur! And you're going to make me sick-ick-ick-ick!"

The sea monster's nasal membranes never so much as twitched.

"It's not wor-wor-wor-orking!" Salem said. "Sto-sto-sto-oppp!"

Sabrina stopped shaking the cat. "It's not working," she admitted.

Captain Cutter scratched his chin. "Maybe we need a more direct application."

"What!?" Sabrina screeched. "You want me to rub my cat in that—that—" She looked at the shiny walls of the nasal passage in front of her and couldn't say it.

"It may be the only way," Captain Cutter said softly.

"No!" Salem bellowed. "No way are you going to rub the cat in that!"

Sabrina took a deep breath. "Okay."

Salem looked at her with wide, fearful, and disbelieving eyes. "No. Not okay. Definitely not okay."

Gritting her teeth, wishing she could point up some gloves, Sabrina pressed the cat against the nasal membrane and started to scour. The cat slid easily.

Salem cried and whimpered, interrupted by the retching noises he made.

At first, Sabrina thought nothing was going to happen. Then she felt Old Agnes shift, tilting her head, then shaking it.

Everyone fell down and struggled to help each other hold on. Water rushed in through the sea monster's open mouth below, sounding like a raging river.

"Into her nose, me hearties!" Captain Cutter commanded. "She's a-gonna blow!"

Chapter 12

Slipping and sliding, Sabrina forced herself into Old Agnes's nasal passage. *This is even worse than when I was in Libby's nose.*

Old Agnes continued moving, obviously in distress. Her nasal passages remained sealed.

"She's a-swimmin' for the surface," Eddie crowed.

"That's because she can't sneeze underwater," Captain Cutter said. "She'd blow her head up tryin'."

And us with it, Sabrina realized. She looked at the closed nasal passages with a mixture of hope and dread. Liquid beaded up on the pink flesh. *Well, sliding through isn't going to be a problem.* She held on to Salem, which was hard, because the cat was so drenched in gross ick that he was slippery as soap.

Then the nasal passage flared open, showing the bright blue sky. A monstrous, windy roar sounded all around Sabrina, and it felt like she'd been seized by a hurricane.

163

AHHHHH-CHOOOOOOO!

Sabrina didn't even have time to think. In the next moment she was flying through the sky. She saw the Sargasso of Lost Ships to one side and *Screamin' Mimi* ahead. Her flight ended abruptly, dumping her into the sea. She went under briefly but started swimming strongly for the pirate ship.

"Swim for it, lads!" Captain Cutter roared out behind her. "Swim for it before Ol' Agnes recovers!"

Unable to stop herself, Sabrina glanced behind and saw that the sea monster was still sneezing. Old Agnes sneezed again and again, unable to pursue. But she did whip up giant waves that curled over the escaping prisoners swimming for *Screamin' Mimi*.

The pirate crew dropped rope ladders into the water. Sabrina grabbed one of them and quickly scrambled up. Salem was right behind her. Once she got on deck, she helped pull the others to safety.

The people living on the Sargasso of Lost Ships cried out for help while Old Agnes continued to sneeze. Sabrina felt terrible watching them.

"Easy, lass," Captain Cutter said gently at her side. "There's naught to be done for the likes o' them right yet. After Ol' Agnes recovers from that sneezin' fit, she's a-gonna be mighty mad. It'd be best if'n we weren't here right then."

"I know."

"An' ye got the word of Captain Cutter that I'll come back and rescue these good folk when we get our other business done. I spent time being a prisoner of that creature. Don't want anybody else a-doin' it."

Sabrina nodded, knowing she had to accept it. Besides, Hilda and Zelda and the crew of *Screamin' Mimi* were depending on them, too.

"Well, lass, now this looks right interestin'," Captain Cutter said.

Sabrina stood in *Screamin' Mimi*'s prow and looked at Queen Becca's flagship. Eddie had taken the coordinates where they were to meet the flagship after escaping Old Agnes. The interesting part Captain Cutter referred to was the other flagship, anchored near Queen Becca's.

"Don't tell me," Sabrina said. "The other ship belongs to King Feargus."

"Aye."

As if I didn't already have enough problems, Sabrina thought tiredly. It had been two days since they'd escaped from Old Agnes. Once Tommy Hawkeyes thought he'd seen her swimming after them, but no one had been sure.

Captain Cutter gave orders to reduce the pirate ship's speed. Slowly, *Screamin' Mimi* came to a halt between the two huge flagships and bobbed on the waves.

"Ahoy, *Screamin' Mimi*," Chatterly called from Queen Becca's flagship. "Did you find the treasure?"

Sabrina saw Chatterly standing beside Queen Becca. The queen didn't look happy. Luckily, most of her attention was directed toward the other ship.

"If you have the treasure," threatened a tall, good-looking man in a crown and robes on the Oot-nannian flagship, "you'll give it to us. Or else."

"Or else?" Sabrina repeated quietly.

"He's obviously not very original," Salem commented. "His threats definitely need improvement."

"But they get the job done all right," Eddie said.

"And that would be King Feargus the Second?" Sabrina asked.

"Aye," Captain Cutter said.

"Don't you dare give the treasure to that low-life, two-timing, would-be Lothario!" Queen Becca screamed.

King Feargus turned toward the queen and leaned out over the railing to scream at her. "Shrew!"

"Nincompoop!" Queen Becca roared back.

"Camel-face!"

The queen gasped angrily and stamped her foot. "You're a wart!" she shouted. "Not only that, but you're an ugly wart! An ugly wart on the south end of a northbound terrlig!"

"Terrlig?" Sabrina asked.

"Kind of a sea skunk," Eddie told her. "Very nasty critters and social outcasts."

King Feargus the Second grabbed the man nearest him and threw him overboard. All the other sailors quickly backed away. The king stomped around for a moment, then leaned back over the railing. "Camel-face!"

"Bellowing barnacle on a blisterfish!"

"Camel-face!"

"Sea scum scraped fresh from a rotting sea scallion!"

"Camel-face!"

Sabrina sighed as she watched the two monarchs continue to scream insults at each other. It was obvious that they had forgotten about her, the treasure, and *Screamin' Mimi* entirely.

"I suppose counseling is out of the question?" she asked Captain Cutter.

"Aye. There's that whole beheadin'-for-failure thing that keeps counselors out of the royal courts."

"Camel-face!" King Feargus the Second shouted.

"Melon-headed, ashy-elbowed, bowlegged, grouper-fish-looking-thing-so-ugly-your-own-mother-wouldn't-love-you piece of pathetic sea cucumber drenched in curdled cod oil!" the queen screamed.

"Well," Sabrina said, "we know which is the more artistic of the two."

In his rage, King Feargus the Second grabbed two more sailors and threw them overboard. The first man was only now climbing back up the side.

"Actually," Captain Cutter said, "when they was together, there was a little bit of peace in these islands. Piratin' was a bit slow, but nothin' you couldn't deal with."

Sabrina hooked her fingers in her mouth and whistled loudly. "Hey, are we going to deal here or not?"

The king and queen both looked back at her.

Captain Cutter coughed delicately and whispered. "Generally, it's not a good thing to interrupt the king and queen while they're a-fightin'."

"I don't have time for their spoiled brat problems," Sabrina said. "There's a guy named Harvey Kinkle back home who spent a miserable Saturday in a basset hound suit selling corn dogs in a mall. I don't know what the time differential is between here and the mortal realm, but I am not about to stand him up."

"Well, I think ye have their attention now."

The queen deliberately faced away from the king, who did the same to her even though he was slower off the mark. Both of them threw their noses into the air and crossed their arms over their chests.

"Do you have the treasure?" the queen demanded.

"Yes," Sabrina replied.

"How do we know you're not lying?"

"Duh," Sabrina said. "Because I couldn't rescue my aunts without it. Do you even know what the treasure is?"

The queen glanced snidely at King Feargus. "We were told that it was a necklace. A very valuable necklace. But we have to consider the source. That person might not have known. Or we may have been lied to. It wouldn't be the first time."

"The necklace is mine," King Feargus the Second responded. "It belonged to my father."

"It still belongs to him," Queen Becca argued. "Ownership doesn't disappear just because you locked him in a tower. We knew we should never have trusted a man who would steal his own father's throne."

"Oh, and you come across so high and mighty," King Feargus the Second said. "And just what part of deep space did you jettison your parents to?"

"They were decrepit," the queen said, "and mentally enfeebled. Come to think of it, you would have been a perfect child for them."

I can't believe this, Sabrina thought. "Guys, hey, guys."

Both monarchs regarded her again.

Sabrina held up the necklace. "I'd really like to have my aunts back."

Queen Becca smiled coldly. "We have your aunts hostage. Chatterly."

Chatterly motioned, and a cargo net was quickly hauled up into the rigging on the queen's flagship. Hilda and Zelda held on to the net.

"Sabrina," Zelda said, "you should have returned to the mortal realm. You shouldn't have come back here."

"I couldn't," Sabrina said. "I would have missed you." *And then there's that whole question of who was going to give me my allowance, allow me to go out with Harvey, etc.*

"She was going to miss us," Hilda said, smiling. "Although you could have saved us all from Willard."

"Hilda, really." Zelda shot her sister a harsh glance.

"Silence!" Queen Becca shouted. Everyone fell silent. "There, that's much better." She turned her attention back to Sabrina. "As you see, we do have your aunts, and unless you give us the necklace, bad things are going to happen to them." She gestured, and a longboat crew beside the flagship started paddling toward *Screamin' Mimi*. "Give these men the necklace and I'll give your aunts back to you."

"Do it," King Feargus the Second threatened, waving his arm, "and I'll blow you out of the water."

Immediately, the Ootnannian artillery crews ran their cannon through the gunports. All of them were pointed at *Screamin' Mimi*.

"Now that," Captain Cutter said quietly, looking down the throats of the nearby cannon, "is a much, much better threat."

"Yeah," Salem agreed.

King Feargus waved again, and a longboat from his flagship started rowing toward the pirate ship.

"Try blowing them out of the water and we'll have you blown out of the water," Queen Becca threatened. She signaled, and her gunports opened, revealing a line of cannon pointed at the Ootnannian flagship.

"Oh yeah, well it'll be the last thing you do." King Feargus the Second signaled, and the deck cannon were shoved up against the railing. All of them pointed at the queen's flagship.

This is so not good, Sabrina realized. The wind blew through her hair, and the smell of brine flooded her nose. If it hadn't been for the fact that her aunts were trapped in a cargo net, that cannon were pointed at her, and that the king and queen were such spoiled brats, it would have been a perfect day for sailing.

"Excuse me," Sabrina interrupted again.

"What?" King Feargus the Second and Queen Becca roared together, sounding terribly agitated.

"Do either of you know what the necklace does?" Sabrina asked.

It was obvious from the looks on their faces that they didn't.

"But you did suspect it was magical in nature, didn't you?" Sabrina asked. "That's why you arranged to meet us here, where the Shield of the Amazing Bob prevents magical spells."

"Get to the point, girl," King Feargus the Second sneered.

"Point," Sabrina repeated. "Actually, that's exactly where I'll start." She pointed at her aunts.

Immediately, Hilda and Zelda disappeared from the cargo net, then reappeared on *Screamin' Mimi*'s deck.

"Sabrina," Hilda said, surprised. "Your powers work."

"Yeah." Sabrina grinned. "Boy, are the king and queen going to be upset. I mean, even more than they are now."

"Not if'n we happen to get blown out of the water by them cannon," Eddie gulped, pointing at all the cannon lined up at them.

"Oh," Sabrina said, "right." *How come there's always so much to remember when you're doing this hero thing?* She pointed quickly and capped all the cannon with corks the way she remembered Aunt Zelda doing.

"Pistols and bows!" King Feargus ordered. "On my mark!"

Ooops. Frantically, Sabrina pointed at the king, then the queen. They disappeared from the decks of their flagships, then reappeared in one of the long-boats standing next to each other. Neither of them looked excited about seeing the other.

"If someone aboard either ship gets trigger-happy," Sabrina warned, "then bad things happen to you." She didn't elaborate on the bad things. Bad things a person imagined were generally worse than things someone told them. Besides, she couldn't make really bad things happen to them and didn't want them to know that.

"She's bluffing," Queen Becca said.

Sabrina pointed, and a beard and mustache grew on the queen's lovely face.

Queen Becca reached up and touched her face. When she understood what had happened, she screamed in terror. "Stop! Stop! We'll do whatever you want!"

King Feargus the Second drew a pistol from under his royal cape.

Sabrina pointed again and altered the king's features, giving him the head of a giant toad.

Toad-face wrinkling in fright, King Feargus the Second dropped his pistol and felt his unlovely face. "No! No!" he wailed in terror.

"Cap'n Polly!" Queen Becca shrieked.

The harsh beating of wings warned Sabrina about the treacherous parrot. Cap'n Polly stretched out a clawed foot, intent on raking the necklace from Sabrina's grasp. Before the bird could take the necklace, however, Salem jumped up in the air and hit Cap'n Polly, knocking her flailing overboard. She plopped into the sea with a big splash.

"Heh heh heh," Salem snickered. "Feather brain."

Squawking angrily, Polly raked her wings through the water and swam to the longboat. Queen Becca ignored her pleas for help, and the parrot had to use her beak and wings to pull herself over the side.

"Neither of those things you did was very nice, Sabrina," Zelda remonstrated.

"I know," Sabrina admitted. "I'm trying really hard not to feel good about it." She raised her voice to the flagship crews. "Throw your weapons overboard if you don't want the same thing to happen to you."

"She can't put a spell on all of us," Chatterly roared. "If we get the necklace back, I'll unspell any of you that need it."

Sabrina turned cold with fear. She hadn't expected that, and it was true that she couldn't put spells on everyone quickly enough.

"If I may," Captain Cutter said, stepping forward and folding his hands together behind his back. "Gun crews port and starboard, pick yer targets and fire on my mark." He glared up at Chatterly.

Chatterly stepped back with a sour look, lowering his sword.

"All rightie then," Captain Cutter said, smiling.

"Milady Sabrina, it appears you have the fates of the two kingdoms in yer hands. What are ye a-gonna do with them?"

Sabrina looked at the king and queen, knowing she couldn't really do anything to them. Still, it didn't seem enough that she'd only freed her aunts. "They should be punished for everything they've done. But that's not up to me."

King Feargus raised a hand, his toad-face purpling with rage. "You're going to regret this, girl. Mark my words, you'll rue this very day."

Without warning, the sea around the longboat suddenly erupted in a spray of waves. Old Agnes surfaced in the middle of the three ships. The sea monster gazed around briefly, her belligerent eyes settling on Sabrina.

The teen witch took Salem in her arms. "Not a good idea. I still have the cat."

Old Agnes snorted in disgust, then turned her attention to the longboat. The bearded queen and toad-faced king held on to each other. Cap'n Polly wrapped her wings around their ankles. All of them quaked in fear. Old Agnes dove on them, gulping them down, quickly disappearing beneath the waves.

Sabrina gazed at the ripples spreading out from where the longboat had been. "Well, I guess maybe that's punishment enough for a while."

"New pictures?"

Sabrina took her thumb from the photograph

she'd just tacked up on the bulletin board in her bedroom.

Harvey Kinkle, looking handsome and not like a basset hound at all, stood in her doorway. "Your aunt Hilda said it was okay if I came on up."

"Sure," Sabrina said, feeling the familiar excitement that she always got after not seeing Harvey for days. Of course, to him it had only been since yesterday, but she'd spent nearly a week in the Other Realm. Once they'd gotten back from rescuing the survivors on the Sargasso of Lost Ships—they'd left King Feargus the Second and Queen Becca with Old Agnes for the time being—she'd barely had enough time for a brief nap. Tonight's date was long overdue.

"So what do you have there?" Harvey stepped closer.

"Oh, just a couple pictures from a trip I took a while back."

"Pirates?" Harvey said, surprised. " 'To Cap'n Sabrina'?"

"Yeah. Cool, huh?"

There were three pictures. One was of Sabrina standing by a cannon with a torch. Another showed her in *Screamin' Mimi*'s crow's nest looking through a spyglass.

The third was her personal favorite, showing her with all of the pirate ship's crew after they'd been rescued from King Feargus the Second's and Queen Becca's dungeons. They held their cutlasses over her head. All of the crew had signed the picture.

"Very cool," Harvey replied. "I used to think

about being a pirate all the time when I was a kid."
He squinted up one eye, closed all the fingers of his
right hand but his forefinger to look like a hook,
and deepened his voice. "Aaaarrrrr, matie."

Sabrina smiled. "Ah, Harvey, they don't really do
that."

"Really?" Harvey looked at the picture again.
"Man, that's disappointing."

"Not really. They do a lot of other piratey things."

"Well, I guess that's good."

"It is. Are you about ready to go? I'm starving
for pizza from the Slicery."

"Sure."

Sabrina grabbed her jacket and headed down-
stairs. They told her aunts good-bye and went out.
The wind was chilly, not at all like what it had been
on the Gentle Sea.

"You know what I like best about pirates?" Harvey asked as he opened the car door.

Sabrina got in. "What?"

"The songs," Harvey said. "You know." He struck
a pirate's pose. "Yo-ho-ho and a bottle of rum.
Pieces-of-eight on a dead man's chest."

"Harvey, stop," Sabrina said anxiously.

Harvey looked at her in confusion.

"No singing," Sabrina said as calmly as she could.

Harvey shrugged. "Sure." He came around the
car and sat behind the wheel.

Sabrina felt guilty. Harvey had worked hard yesterday even though it had been a week ago to her,
and he probably needed to let off some steam.

"Well," she said, trying not to sound reluctant, "maybe one song."

Harvey grinned as he drove. "I know just the song. It's really easy. You can learn it quick." He cleared his throat. "Ninety-nine bottles of ale on the wall, ninety-nine bottles of ale—"

Despite the fact that she was tired of the song after all the time spent with the pirates, Sabrina couldn't help but get pulled along by Harvey's enthusiasm. "Take one down and pass it around, ninety-eight bottles of ale on the wall."

After all, there was no one she'd rather sing with than Harvey Kinkle. Even silly pirate songs.

About the Author

Mel Odom lives in Moore, Oklahoma, with his wife and five children. He's the author of three other *Sabrina, the Teenage Witch* books. He has also written books for *Buffy the Vampire Slayer, The Secret World of Alex Mack, The Journey of Allen Strange, Young Hercules,* and the novelization of *Snow Day.* He coaches basketball, baseball, and football and loves watching his kids play sports. When not at a game or writing, he's known to hang out on the Internet until way after the cows come home. He can be reached at denimbyte@aol.com.

Put a little magic in your everyday life!

Magic Handbook

Patricia Barnes-Svarney

Sabrina has a Magic Handbook, full of spells and rules to help her learn to control her magic. Now you can have your own Magic Handbook, full of tricks and everyday experiments you can do to find the magic that's inside and all around you!

From Archway Paperbacks
Published by Pocket Books

2021-02

***A fun-filled guide
to the mystery and
magic of the universe!***

*Sabrina's Guide
to the Universe*

Using my magic, Salem and I traveled
through outer space and now we want
to share our discoveries with you!

by
Patricia Barnes-Svarney

**From Archway Paperbacks
Published by Pocket Books**

2316